A pretty flush crept over her face. "I want to spend a little time with you. Get to know you better." He cocked his head, wanting to make sure he'd heard right. "I think you've got potential, Eagle Scout. I want to find out for sure."

This wasn't a declaration of undying love, but it was still one of the best things he'd ever heard. "Come here," he said, weak with relief as he reached for her.

They came together in front of his desk. The second he touched her, all his stern personal admonitions and ideas about not overwhelming her went right out his floor-to-ceiling windows. Holding her face between his hands, he burrowed his fingers into the heavy satin of her hair, feeling for the warmth of her scalp underneath. There was time for only two words before he angled her head back, bent his face down and kissed her.

"Thank you."

Their mouths fit together, tentative at first, a slow, testing slide of lips so they could get the feel of each other and get past the electric sensation of being in each other's arms.

And then his mind blanked out and his body took over.

Part of it was that she was so fragrant—flowers and coconuts; he'd missed that heady combination—and so soft and yielding an  ldcat. Plus, she made thes at shot straight to the im. Whatever. The poi le.

He was always losir

Books by Ann Christopher

Harlequin Kimani Romance

Just About Sex
Sweeter Than Revenge
Tender Secrets
Road to Seduction
Campaign for Seduction
Redemption's Kiss
Seduced on the Red Carpet
Redemption's Touch
The Surgeon's Secret Baby
Sinful Seduction
Sinful Temptation
Case for Seduction
Sinful Attraction
Sinful Paradise

ANN CHRISTOPHER

is a full-time chauffeur for her two overscheduled children. She is also a wife, former lawyer and decent cook. In between trips to various sporting practices and games, Target and the grocery store, she likes to write the occasional romance novel. She lives in Cincinnati and spends her time with her family, which includes two spoiled rescue cats, Sadie and Savannah, and two rescue hounds, Sheldon and Dexter. As always, Ann is hard at work on her next book, and hopes that—if you haven't already—you'll pick up the first three books in her Davies Legacy series, *Sinful Seduction, Sinful Temptation* and *Sinful Attraction,* which are still available.

If you'd like to recommend a great book, share a recipe for homemade cake of any kind, or have a tip for getting your children to do what you say the *first* time you say it, Ann would love to hear from you through her website, www.annchristopher.com.

Sinful
PARADISE

Ann Christopher

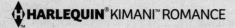

HARLEQUIN® KIMANI™ ROMANCE

To Richard

Recycling programs
for this product may
not exist in your area.

ISBN-13: 978-0-373-86352-5

SINFUL PARADISE

HARLEQUIN®
™ www.Harlequin.com

Printed in U.S.A.

Dear Reader,

If you've been following my Davies Legacy series, you know that Cooper Davies has felt a sharp interest in Gloria Adams ever since he first laid eyes on her in *Sinful Temptation*. You also know that he pined after her in *Sinful Attraction* but wasn't able to jumpstart their relationship, much to his bitter disappointment. Ever wonder what happened between them the night he took her home from the gala, or why he was so depressed the night of the big auction?

Well, you're about to find out!

I've saved their story for last. I had a great time writing it and putting them through the wringer on their way to happily-ever-after, and I sure hope you think I did them justice....

Happy reading!

Ann

Chapter 1

One Year Ago

Cooper Davies crossed his ankles, leaned against the bar's marble countertop and scanned the black-tie crowd. Scowled. Checked his watch. Scanned the crowd again, which was, by his rough count, the ten millionth time he'd done so in the past hour.

There was still no sign of her.

"Shit," he muttered, killing the rest of his bourbon. Then he thunked the empty tumbler down in front of the bartender, who stopped slicing lemons long enough to eye him with concern. "Hit me again."

"You might want to slow down, chief," the bartender said.

Cooper fished a fifty out of his pocket and dropped

it into the tip jar. "To thank you for putting a lid on the advice while you pour," he said with a tight smile. "And I prefer to be called boss."

The bartender shrugged and reached for the bourbon bottle. "Whatever you say, boss."

"Appreciate it," Cooper told him.

Why wasn't she here by now? he wondered moodily, taking his refilled tumbler, moving into the crowd and going through the appropriate social motions. He nodded at an elderly woman whose neck was weighed down with so many diamonds he wondered how she was able to breathe and shook his head at a passing server who offered him a lamb chop from his silver tray.

Cooper barely saw either of them. His relentless focus was on one thing and one thing only: Gloria Adams.

She had to be here somewhere, right? She wouldn't want to miss her sister's big night, would she? No. So she'd be there.

But—terrible new thought—what if she was out of town?

His gut gave a sickening lurch and leveled out somewhere near his ankles.

No. She'd be there. He just needed to be patient.

Ha. As if he could be.

He and patience had rarely occupied the same room.

"Not bad, eh?" His adopted brother, Marcus Davies, materialized by his side and raised his voice over the crowd's dull roar and the pianist's plinking on the concert grand in the corner of the soaring atrium. "Talia's got skills."

Staring up at the twenty-foot mural, Cooper nodded. It was the focal point of this whole overblown shindig at their family's Manhattan auction house, Davies & Sons, which he co-owned and ran with Marcus. Their cousin Tony Davies and his brother, Sandro, were also co-owners. Talia Adams was the artist who'd revitalized the building, and so she was tonight's guest of honor.

"Agreed," Cooper said.

"We've got skills, too," Marcus said. "We can pull a crowd."

"Yep," Cooper said absently, craning his neck and scanning heads. Maybe Gloria'd gone into the ladies' room....

"And maybe you need to get your head out of your ass."

"True," Cooper said.

A beat passed.

"Wait, what?" Cooper said, giving his brother a sidelong glare.

"What's your issue?" Marcus asked, eyes glinting with amusement. "You keep looking around like you're in the middle of a game of Where's Waldo? Who'd you lose?"

The problem with brothers, Cooper thought, was that they noticed shit. Especially the shit you wanted boxed up and stored in a dark corner of your locked closet, never to see the light of day.

"Am I supposed to know what you're talking

about?" Cooper tried to bank some of the intensity he was feeling, working hard to smooth out the lines that had to be grooving across his forehead. He'd never had much of a poker face. "Or is this just random blathering?"

Marcus, realizing he'd struck a nerve, even if he didn't know which one, grinned. "Keep drinking like that. I'll get it out of you."

He probably would, Cooper silently agreed.

Bottoming out this latest bourbon, Cooper glanced around to see how far he was from the bar and how many people he'd have to tackle to get there—

There she was! Coming out of the ladies' room with Talia, just as he'd thought! She was here! Right over there, with her back to him, talking to her sister! A crazy combination of excitement and nerves swooped through him, drying out his mouth and making his heart thud.

"And in a complete change of topic," Marcus was saying, "remind me to tell you what Johnson said about..."

Cooper didn't give a damn about what Johnson, their building manager, or anyone else said about anything. Not when Gloria Adams was in the room.

Without another word, he thrust his empty glass at his startled brother and wove his way through the crowd. In a monumental feat of self-control, he managed to resist the urge to elbow people out of his way. Afraid she'd disappear before he could get to her, he stared at her to the exclusion of everything else, letting the promise of her reel him in like a caught marlin.

Man, she was something.

Her body was long and lean, willowy but curved where it counted, and it was poured into a slinky black number that was sleeveless and backless, draped along the sides of her toned back and dipping just low enough to taunt him with the flare of her ass, which was rounded and tight. The crowd shifted, giving him a quick glimpse of her legs, which were long and bare, and her spiky screw-me-now heels.

Desire swelled, hard and hot, deep in his belly.

And lower.

He wanted her. He wanted to take the two sides of that expensive black dress, right where they skimmed across her shoulders, and rip it down the middle so he could get to that body. He wanted to run his tongue down that spine and bite that ass. He wanted those legs wrapped around his waist and then propped against his shoulders, and he wanted to take her and take her and take her…until neither of them could move and they'd both forgotten their own names.

He wanted her mouth, her lips. Wanted to kiss, suck and bite them, and then he wanted them running and licking all up and down his body, and then—oh, yeah—he wanted those big lips to suck him off as she took his hardened length as deep into her mouth as he could go and he slid his fingers into the thick silk of her shiny black hair.

And then he wanted it all again.

He'd thought and dreamed of nothing else since their first—and only—meeting a few weeks ago, when he'd met her at Talia's studio and they'd said hello to each other. That was the sum total of his interaction with her, despite his lingering interest, and he'd been debating what to do about it. The relentlessness of his wanting concerned him a little bit, to be honest, because he'd never felt anything like it. If anyone had asked him his preferred type of woman five minutes before he met Gloria, he'd've sworn up and down that it was petite blondes with big tits.

And now?

Now things had changed. Big-time.

If he needed any further proof of that, it came when she turned just slightly, and her high-cheeked, straight-nosed profile was bleak, if not distraught. When she wiped her eyes with a tissue, his muscles bunched up and his nerves tightened down, and the protective, problem-solving section of his brain, which was about half to three-quarters, kicked into overdrive.

Did she need him to solve something for her? Fix it? Kill it?

Because he would. For Gloria? You bet he would.

And that was problematic. Because he didn't know her from Eve, and he sure as hell wasn't the white-knight type.

White? Yeah. Knight? Not so much.

"Ladies," he said, coming abreast of them, "is something wrong?"

Startled, they turned to face him, and his gaze locked with Gloria's. Her eyes widened with shock and then swept him up and down with subtle feminine appreciation, generating a pulse of electricity that seemed to dance across his skin.

He'd forgotten the fine details of her face, or maybe it was that his overwhelmed brain couldn't catalog all of her intriguing features. The almond-shaped eyes in blackest brown, a color so pure and crystalline that he felt sure he could stare into them for several fascinating hours without blinking. The sleek cheekbones, flushed with color. The plump...sexy...delicious curve of her full lips. Her amazing lips.

He wanted her with a vehemence that worried him—seriously made him wonder what the hell he'd gotten into—but he had bigger problems than that.

Gloria had been crying, and the telltale makeup smudges under her eyes made him long to see her dimpled smile again even more than he wanted to screw her.

And that was a whole freaking lot.

Some of his intensity must have shown on his face, because Gloria's eyes widened and he heard the slight hitch of her breath. Then she pulled out a compact and went to work powdering her nose, dismissing him without a word.

This rudeness seemed to embarrass Talia, who shot her sister a glare. "Gloria has, ah, decided to leave the party—"

"No, I haven't," Gloria interjected loudly.

Another glare. "And I'm going to throw her into a cab and send her home, so we're all good. Thanks."

Cooper frowned, wondering when he'd heard a worse idea. Set Gloria loose in midtown with all those men? In that dress? Not on his watch. "I don't think she should go anywhere by herself."

"I know," Talia agreed, "but I can't leave the party yet, and I'm not sure—"

"I can see her home," Cooper said quickly.

"—that I can... Wait, what?"

"I can see her home," Cooper repeated.

Talia hesitated. "Well…"

Dark amusement almost made him smile. Talia was no dummy, clearly, and he was having a hard time keeping a lid on his attraction to Gloria. If Talia knew the kinds of things he wanted to do with her sister, she'd probably prefer to send Gloria off in a gypsy cab and give the driver instructions to take her directly to a Times Square bar.

"She's with me," he reassured Talia, playing at that white-knight crap again. Where the hell was that coming from? "Don't worry."

"I'm not sure you're safe with her, frankly," Talia muttered.

Cooper laughed. He could only wish.

Gloria closed her compact with a snap and tuned into the conversation for the first time. "What's the plan? Who's coming to the bar with me?"

"You're not going to the bar," Talia said flatly. "Cooper's taking you home."

"Taking me home?" Gloria asked, and there was a husky new note in her voice that made heat pool in his belly.

Which made him a rotten bastard because she'd been crying at a black-tie event and drinking heavily—

he could smell the lingering fruitiness of champagne on her breath—two signs that pointed to man trouble.

Which meant that Gloria was wounded and vulnerable right now and would probably regret whatever she said tonight when the cold light of day hit her tomorrow. And he didn't want any part of Gloria's regret. He'd take anything else she wanted to give him, but not her regret.

"Making sure you get home," he clarified, taking her elbow. "Ready?"

"Hang on. Thanks, Cooper. You're a lifesaver." Rising on her tiptoes, Talia whispered in his ear under the guise of kissing his cheek. "And if you take advantage of my sister while she's drunk, I'm going to clip your balls, fry them up in a beer batter and serve them to you with hot sauce. *Comprende?*"

This time he did laugh. "Oh, I *comprende*. And since my balls are very important to me, you won't have to worry about me taking advantage of Gloria." That would have been the perfect time to shut the hell up, but a sudden wave of seriousness hit him. For some inexplicable reason, he wanted them both to trust him. "Ever," he added.

Looking reassured, Talia nodded and moved aside.

But Gloria, who'd been watching Cooper's little speech with narrow-eyed suspicion, swiped at her eyes again and told Talia something that felt like a fist directly to Cooper's gut. "Learn from my mistakes, okay, Tally? Don't bother counting on a man. They never come through in the end."

Chapter 2

Gloria's words were still buzzing unpleasantly inside Cooper's head when he steered her out to the curb, where the limo he'd hired for the night was waiting for them. So it was man trouble, then, just as he'd suspected. Some man had made Gloria cry.

Sudden moodiness weighed him down as he opened the door for her and watched her slide across the seat, crossing her legs and smoothing her skirt as she went. He climbed in after her and slammed the door shut harder than he'd meant to, cocooning them in an intimate world of leather lit only by the city's lights outside their blacked-out windows.

Gloria didn't trust men.

The driver, lit by the dome light, cocked his head, waiting.

"SoHo." Gloria gave him the full address. "Thanks— Wait, sir." There was a sudden sharp concern in Gloria's voice that drew Cooper's full attention. "You have a growth on your jaw. Back by your ear."

"Yeah," the guy said sheepishly, rubbing the spot, which didn't look any too good. "I keep meaning to get it checked out. You know how it is. No time with the job and running the kids all over the place."

"How long has it been there?" Gloria demanded.

The guy shrugged. "Six months? A year? I lose track. My annual's coming up in a few months—"

"I'm a physician," Gloria told him. "I'm very concerned about this spot. *Very concerned.* Please get it checked out first thing Monday."

The guy stiffened, then bristled, waving a hand. "It's nothing. I'll get to it—"

Gloria made a dismissive noise. "You don't have a wife, do you?"

"How'd you know that?"

"Because she'd've been all over your butt about getting that checked out before now."

The driver quieted down, looking disgruntled.

Gloria, pressing her advantage, reached out and squeezed the guy on the shoulder. "You want your kids to have their father around for a good long time, don't you?"

He nodded.

"Then take care of yourself, okay?"

Another nod.

"Monday— What's your name?"

"Bruce," he said dully.

"Monday, Bruce. No excuses. This is the most important thing you can do right now."

Another nod, this time with a half smile, although the poor guy was definitely looking shaky. "Thanks." Bruce hesitated, taking a deep breath. "Well, I'd better get you folks home, eh?" He hit a button and disappeared behind the smooth whoosh of the glass divider.

Gloria settled back against her seat and buckled up.

Cooper watched her, feeling a little dazed as he added brains and compassion to the list of things she had going for her. "Nice work, Doctor."

She looked out her window, presenting him with her profile. "Just another day at the office."

"Still nice work."

She shot him a quick, sad look and kept her voice low. "In another six months, there won't be much they can do for him. I figure children need their father for as long as possible."

"Agreed."

"Are you a daddy, Cooper?"

"Not yet. It's high on my list, though. I'm not getting any younger."

One of her brows arched. "Who is?"

Here in their private world, he felt as if he should tell her a few things about himself—the kinds of things he normally skimmed over when dating someone new. "I got married right out of college. Lasted a couple years. People call them starter marriages now, but that's not how I saw it."

"What happened?"

"She didn't want kids. Or anything else that interfered with her social life and me time." He paused. "Which meant she didn't really want a husband."

"That's funny." Her lips curled into a bleak smile. "My starter marriage ended because my husband didn't see why he needed to stop screwing other women."

"We sure can pick 'em, eh?"

"Yeah," she said. Something closed off in her expression as she turned back to her window and stared fixedly out of it. "We sure can."

That should have been a good time to keep quiet, but some elusive yet insistent impulse spurred him on. "We need to do much better next time, don't we, Gloria?"

She didn't answer.

The car finally pulled away from the curb and into the heavy traffic. Cooper rested an elbow on his window and stared at the passing buildings, his entire being divided into two halves. One half reveled in the long stretch of Gloria's shapely legs, right there within touching distance. He could sense the solid warmth of her body—she smelled like some exotic tropical flower with a mouthwatering hint of coconut thrown in—and the slow rise and fall of her small breasts as she breathed. His other half wondered what had happened tonight to deepen her mistrust of men—*Learn from my mistakes,* she'd told her sister. He decided that she'd damn sure learn to trust him.

Which made no sense, right?

Because this was good news, wasn't it? She didn't

trust men; ergo, she wasn't living with someone or engaged and was therefore free to hook up with Cooper. Trust, he knew from long experience, was of marginal importance when it came to hookups. Sure, you had to trust your partner to practice safe sex and give you a few orgasms, but beyond that, who the hell cared? He'd had some of the best sex of his life in situations where trust never even crossed his mind. Things like flexibility, endurance and willingness to experiment had been far more important to him.

And now...

"Why'd you leave your own party to take me home?" Gloria asked, startling him.

He turned to face her, caught in the bright gleam of her eyes and the throatiness of her voice. It took him a couple of long beats to speak, during which she shifted restlessly, uncrossing and recrossing her legs.

"I wanted to make sure you got home safe," he finally said.

Her lips thinned as though she'd expected him to have more faith in her. "I'm a grown woman and a lifelong New Yorker. What could happen?"

He gave her a lingering once-over that was, when he thought about it later, pretty blatant. "With you? Upset and crying? In that dress?" He shook his head, muttering darkly. "Sky's the limit."

She smiled crookedly and gave her chin a defiant hitch. "True. But it's my sky and my limit."

He stared at her, irritated and not liking the sound of that. "Since you're not so hot at looking after yourself at the moment, consider me a volunteer to do it for you."

"And why would you do that?" she demanded.

"Because I want to."

"Why?"

Her gaze was direct. Suspicious.

And maybe a little intrigued, he realized, a discovery that made heat flare across his cheeks.

Because there was no good answer to her question—none that he was willing to give, anyway—he changed the subject to the topic he knew he'd be wondering about far into the future if he didn't ask.

"I don't want to get into it now. Why were you crying?"

"That's an incredibly personal question."

"True. But I feel like someone owes me an explanation. I'm taking a beautiful woman home after a party, but I don't get to sleep with her. My whole universe is out of whack."

A flicker of amusement lit her eyes, but she didn't smile. "I'm grateful for the ride. Sort of. I wasn't really done drinking for the night, but it's all good. I have wine at home. So thanks. But my personal life is still none of your business."

They'd see about that, he thought sourly.

"Where's your date, anyway?" she asked.

He frowned. "Isn't that a personal question? Did you change your mind about conversation topics already?"

"If your personal life is also off-limits, I'm sure

you'll say so. But that wasn't really a personal question, was it? It's more logistics."

She had him there; he wasn't about to start throwing up boundaries between them, especially when she was already doing such a great job at it.

"I'm not dating anyone right now. Why're you looking at me like that?"

Her brows had shot up. "You're so full of it. Men are always with someone. And they usually have someone else on speed dial, so don't bullshit me. I'm speaking from painful experience."

"I'm not bullshitting you. I'll never bullshit you."

She turned her cool profile to him and looked out her window. "It doesn't matter whether you are or not. We'll probably never see each other again after tonight anyway."

"Oh, we'll see each other again," he said. "I promise you that."

That brought her head back around in a hurry.

They stared at each other for one hard pregnant moment that ended only when she wavered and looked away first, which he considered a victory. A small victory, since he wasn't sleeping with her tonight, but he'd take what he could get.

She shifted with restless energy, then leaned forward and reached for the minibar. "Is there anything to drink in this expensive—? Oh, good. Vodka. Not my favorite, but I'll take it."

"Haven't you had enough for tonight?"

"Not even close," she said flatly.

"Great," he said, watching her reach for a crystal

tumbler. "Help yourself. The thing to remember when you've finished puking your guts out in the morning is that you need three raw eggs chased with a full tablespoon of hot sauce. People always try to skimp on the hot sauce. If you follow my directions, you should feel human again by noon or so."

She looked at the tumbler in her hand, gave the vodka one last lingering glance, then slammed it back down, closed the minibar door and, with a disgruntled huff, leaned back against the seat and resumed her moody staring out the window.

Another small victory for him, he thought with grim satisfaction.

They rode in silence for a minute or two. Traffic was bad tonight, meaning he had plenty of time to watch the way passing lights flickered over her cheekbones...her shapely shoulders and arms...the gentle curves of her breasts...the delicious gleam of her skin.

His blood felt as if it was heating and thickening, slowly spreading desire to every corner of his body.

"So why aren't you dating anyone?" she quietly asked after a while.

He waited, saving his answer until she hesitantly— reluctantly—turned her gaze back to his. He saw the subtle increase in the rise and fall of her breasts.

"I have my eye on someone." If the telltale huskiness in his voice didn't give him away, the way he was looking at her surely would. He was calling on every ounce of self-control to stop himself from reaching for her. "I'll let her know when the time is right."

She stared at him.

Several beats passed.

Time may have stopped.

"And when will that be?" she asked.

He shrugged, his face hot. "Up to her."

She tried to smile, but only one corner of her mouth lifted. "Men aren't known for their patience."

"You don't know everything about men, Gloria. And some things are worth waiting for."

"And this woman is?"

"Absolutely."

She hesitated. Blinked. Opened and shut her mouth. Tried again. "And what do you see in this woman, pray tell?"

That was easy.

"Everything." He paused. "I wish she saw it, too."

She immediately seemed to regret asking the question. Some of her bravado crumpled and fell with her expression. Her chin trembled, forcing her to press her lips together. He was just beginning to wonder if he'd made her cry again when her phone pinged.

With a quick swipe at her eyes, she fished it out of her beaded bag, looked at the display and hissed— actually bared her teeth and made a sound like a striking snake.

Alarmed, he gave up all pretext of being a polite human being, craned his neck and read her private text, praying she wouldn't notice. Luckily, she was too focused on Aaron's words to see what he was doing. *Aaron.* Now he knew who his enemy was.

I'm sorry, baby, it said. Are you home? If I can get away, I want to see you so we can talk.

Through the red haze of his sudden anger, Cooper tried to piece together the whole picture.

It was now—he checked his watch—twelve-thirty, and *Aaron,* who hadn't taken this incredibly sexy woman to the gala and had also made her cry, now wanted to show up at her crib, for talking. *Talking.* Which Cooper knew, as all men did, was code for *booty call.*

So...

Aaron was either married, or he was the stupidest punk to ever climb out of the primordial ooze and walk on two legs—probably both.

Either way, Cooper wanted to rip the man's throat out for putting that look of despairing rage on Gloria's face.

What the hell was he supposed to do now? He opened his mouth, hoping inspiration was on its way.

"Gloria," he began.

She lowered her window just as the car rolled to a stop at a light. Without a word, she threw her cell phone out the window with all her might. It connected with the sidewalk, and Cooper saw it splinter into several pieces before the window whooshed back up and the car started moving again.

Astonished, he watched as she wiped her hands together as though she was getting rid of chalk dust, leaned toward the minibar again and reached for the vodka.

This time he didn't try to stop her as she poured herself a drink.

* * *

By the time they pulled up to her brownstone on a quiet tree-lined street ten minutes later, she'd downed about three fingers of vodka and he'd helped himself to the bourbon, which meant that neither of them was feeling any pain. Unless you counted his raging hormones, which felt as though they were poisoning his judgment way more than the liquor was.

Still, he was determined to do the right thing tonight.

Assuming he could remember what that was.

He opened the door and climbed out, catching Gloria's warm hand and helping her out after him. The light breeze felt refreshingly cool against his overheated face, but nowhere near as good as the slide of her soft palm against his. And then she was out of the limo, a little unsteady in her spiky heels, and there was nothing else for him to do but hang on to her, his hands low on her supple hips, and make sure she didn't stumble.

Jesus.

His breath and his heart met in his throat, nearly choking him with lust. There was no way his lungs could function when she was this close—when all he had to do was contract his arms and she'd be fully up against his body, and a simple lowering of his chin would connect his mouth to hers.

And she was willing. More than willing. Her fragrant body was alight beneath his fingers, a living flame ready to be stoked and stroked into an inferno.

Her raspy breath singed his neck, and when she spoke, her lips whispered across his skin.

"You want me."

A shaky laugh. To keep himself from kissing her mouth, after which he knew he'd be lost, he pressed his lips to her forehead.

"Yeah. I want you."

She eased closer. "You can have me," she said urgently.

"I will have you," he promised her. "Just not tonight. I'm not down with being used so you can forget some other man who doesn't deserve you anyway. Or taking advantage of women who've had too much to drink. But I don't want you to have any questions about it—I plan to take you up on that offer."

Gloria didn't like this. She snatched her body free, taking heaven with her and leaving him empty-handed and agitated.

"You're assuming the offer will be open after tonight," she snapped over her shoulder as she hurried up the steps to the front door.

Great, he thought, scrubbing a hand over his face in frustration.

Now he'd offended her.

Her strides were long, but his were longer. He caught up with her just as she unlocked the door, which was heavy and ornate with beveled glass, and put his hand over hers on the brass knob.

"Gloria," he tried.

She looked down at his hand engulfing hers, her muscles tense.

He reluctantly pulled his hand away.

"Thank you for bringing me home," she said formally, not looking at him. "You're a good guy."

"No, I'm not. I just don't want to see regret in your eyes when you look at me."

Her gaze flickered up to his then, so glittering and bright it was like looking into the heart of the universe. Tears gleamed in her brown eyes and fringed her thick lashes, and his breath caught when her expression softened into a near smile.

"No regrets." Those amazing eyes crinkled at the corners. "That'd be a nice change for me."

"Good to hear." Reaching out, he rubbed his thumb under her eye, catching one of her tears and sucking it into his mouth. She watched him, gasping quietly. "'Cause I'm already regretting not throwing you over my shoulder and taking you upstairs." He sighed harshly. "I really regret it. I'd have you naked by now, in case you were wondering."

She grinned and dropped her gaze, blushing, and the contrast between this Gloria and the sad one of ten seconds ago was dizzying.

"You don't know," he said on a shaky laugh, running his fingers through his hair and ruffling it, determined to keep his hands occupied so he wouldn't reach for her again. "You have no idea."

A line grooved down her forehead. "What?"

"How beautiful you are. How much I've wanted you since the second I saw you."

"Tonight?"

"No." He paused, giving this information time to

sink in. When her eyes widened, he continued. "The second I met you."

She slowly shook her head. "I didn't know."

"Now you do."

They stared at each other, the door still open between them, her hand still on the knob.

His gaze drifted to her lips. They were lush and dewy, things of beauty to be kissed, licked and savored, and he wanted to taste them. Really wanted to taste them.

Breathless, she tipped her chin up, her eyes closing.

He drifted closer, his lids feeling heavy, as though he'd been drugged, and his hands started to come up to hold her face between his hands.

Catching himself and hanging on to his determination to do the right thing by a frayed thread, he diverted his hands by running them both through his hair, pulling at his roots a little because he seemed to need an infusion of pain to clear his head.

She also seemed to come to her senses and took a step away from him.

"Yeah," he said hoarsely. "Yeah, so…I'd better… I'll just get…" He trailed off like an idiot, gesturing vaguely over his shoulder toward the limo.

She blinked and nodded, further breaking the spell between them. "You have to go."

"I should go," he agreed, even though he'd willingly pay a million dollars and sacrifice a couple of his lesser toes to stay. "Yeah. I'm gonna go."

Galvanized by the sudden awkwardness of the situation, he strode off and was halfway back down the steps to the street before he realized he probably didn't want to leave things like that. There were a few important details he needed to nail down, like getting her number and making sure he'd see her again sometime soon. But this was what this woman did to him—she reduced him to a mindless idiot.

Cursing under his breath, he wheeled back around, praying she was still there.

"The thing is," he began with a laugh as casual as he could make it, "I was wondering—"

"Coffee," she said at the same time. "I mean—do you drink coffee?"

"I live for coffee."

There was a pause.

"Good." Nodding decisively, she stepped aside and held the door open for him.

Abandoning all pretext of being casual, he took the steps three at a time, ridiculously grateful for any excuse to extend tonight's interlude with her.

Chapter 3

They walked through the lobby and rode the elevator to the second floor in silence. The place was understated and elegant, with dark paneling, Oriental rugs, gilt mirrors, sconces and fresh flower arrangements in all the common areas. There was only one other apartment on her floor, he realized, feeling the pleasant kick of anticipation as she opened the door and let them in, clicking on the lights as she went.

He wanted to know everything there was to know about her, and he wanted to know it now.

"Nice digs," he said, taking it all in with a sweeping gaze.

That was an understatement.

In sharp contrast to the old-money feel of the rest of the building, Gloria's apartment was all modern decor, with boxy black leather sectionals, ottomans and chairs, sleek chrome accents, glass tables, mirrors and a wicked zebra-print rug that probably cost the Earth with a couple of minor planets thrown in. It was a straight stretch from foyer to kitchen, with living and dining areas between and the glittering lights of nighttime Manhattan on the other side of the sheer drapes. There were occasional pops of color in the accent pillows, flowers and sculptures, all of which seemed to take their inspiration from the vivid paintings on the walls.

"Thanks," she said. "I'm not sure how much longer I'll be here."

"Why? Rent going up?"

"No. The city is wearing me out. I need more space. More grass. Might be time for me to move to the suburbs."

He stared at her, his thoughts emptying out.

"What?" she asked, arrested.

"I just bought a fixer-upper in Greenwich. For those reasons. I'm having it renovated before I move in."

"Oh," she said, a faint frown marring her forehead.

After an awkward silence, he nodded to the painting over the fireplace, a study of orange, red and blue that fed the space's energy. "Talia's work. She's good."

"Damn good," Gloria agreed, kicking off her heels and tossing her keys in a basket on a hall console as she passed. "Free paintings are one of the perks of having a sister who's an artist."

"Do you play?" He nodded at the concert-sized grand in front of the curtained windows.

"Absolutely." She grinned and counted on her fingers. "So far I've mastered 'Chopsticks,' 'Twinkle, Twinkle' and 'Mary Had a Little Lamb.' Well worth the two years of lessons I've shelled out for. The neighbors are asleep, or I'd give you a concert. I can almost always manage to play with both hands."

He grinned back. "Impressive."

"I strive. Do you play?"

"Hell, no. And your OCD looks like it's worse than mine, by the way. This is some kitchen."

He followed her into it, afraid to touch any of the gleaming surfaces for fear he'd leave an unwanted fingerprint somewhere. In a city full of tiny galley kitchens where you could hardly open the refrigerator door without banging it into the oven, she had a full-sized kitchen with stainless-steel appliances and a six-burner stove that looked as if it could manage dinner for the whole building in ten minutes or less.

Gloria laughed and went to work on the cappuccino machine. "Here's a shameful secret—I don't cook."

Cooper narrowed his eyes at her and focused on broaching this important subject carefully. "By *don't,* you mean…?"

"Can't. I can't cook."

"And by *can't,* you mean…?"

"I ain't got no skills, Cooper."

"And by *no,* you mean…?"

"I order in, okay! Or I bring it home from the hospital cafeteria! Or I eat cereal."

He pressed a hand to his temple and shook his head as he leaned against the black granite counter. "I need to sit down for that kind of information. This is sad, Gloria. I am saddened. Deeply saddened."

"I know."

"You don't seem to care about this deficiency."

"I don't care. I have no desire to cook."

"Give me a minute. I'm dizzy."

"So...are you a caveman, or is it a time warp and you think it's still 1950, or—? What exactly is your objection here?"

"I think everyone should embrace the joys of cooking a home meal. Men and women alike."

Gloria looked around, arrested, measuring spoon poised over the coffee. "So you cook, then."

"I'm a great cook. In fact—are you hungry? I'd love an omelet right about now." He walked to the fridge, opened it and peered inside. "Maybe with some mushrooms—aaand maybe not. There's nothing in your fridge other than pomegranate juice and Dijon mustard. I can't cook an omelet with that. Omelets require eggs. I'm going to give you several demerits in my ongoing marriageable-woman assessments. Do you have anything frozen that I can defrost and—? Hey, what's wrong?" He straightened and let the fridge door slam shut, food forgotten. She had a hand pressed to her belly, and her expression was so stricken and forlorn that he wondered if she was in pain.

"Gloria?"

She looked away, her gaze darting to the cabinets... to the coffeemaker...anywhere but him.

"I've never had a man in this great apartment before, unless you count the maintenance guy and the painters." She shook her head and worked at a wry smile, failing miserably. "I've never had a man offer to cook me anything. Not even microwave popcorn." Her lips twisted; then she laughed derisively. The sound was so bitter and brittle that he winced away from it, wishing he could cover his ears. "And I'm a really stupid person. Just so you know."

That was going way too far, no matter what else was happening in her life.

"You're not stupid," he said flatly.

"Don't be so sure."

The unshakable certainty in her voice angered him. "You're not—"

"Yeah, okay, you're right." She swiped her nose with the back of her hand and finally met his gaze, her eyes a hard glitter of self-hatred. "I'm book smart. We can agree on that. I'm an NYU-trained plastic surgeon who put herself through school and makes damn good money. I'm good with nose jobs and breast augmentations. If you need your chin lifted, I'm your woman. But in my personal life? Where it counts?" That bitter laugh again. "I'm too stupid to live."

"Gloria—"

"But the good news is," she added brightly, "that I'm just smart enough to be grateful you didn't let me compound my stupidity by having sex with a near-complete stranger, even though I wanted to. So thanks again." Her face crumpled, killing him slowly as he watched her, but he forced himself not to reach for her now because he knew she'd fall apart and hate him later for it. "Can you let yourself out? I really need to—" She gestured helplessly over her shoulder, pointing to the hallway. "I really need to go to bed."

With that, she clapped a hand over her mouth and raced off, disappearing down the long hallway in a swish of fragrant silk and slamming the bedroom door behind her.

Well, shit, Cooper thought, feeling flummoxed and clumsy as he watched her go. He took one hurried step after her, caught himself, held his hands out in a hopeless gesture to no one in particular and finished, lamely, by collapsing on the nearest ottoman and cursing under his breath.

What the hell was he supposed to do now?

Leave?

Yeah, no. That wasn't going to work. He didn't think Gloria'd ever hurt herself or anything, but he didn't know her well and he definitely didn't like her state of mind. She was hurting and her hurt had inexplicably become his hurt. He wasn't going to walk out on her in a dark moment, even if she wanted him to. He rubbed a hand over his knotted gut, wishing he could loosen up some of his tight muscles.

So…yeah. He was here for a while. He'd give her a few minutes to calm down. Then he'd try to talk to her, maybe see if he could somehow help. He could volunteer to smash Aaron's face to smithereens. He'd be happy to help with that.

Meanwhile, he decided, shrugging out of his jacket, untucking his shirt, rolling up his sleeves and kicking off his shoes, he might as well make himself comfortable.

Where was the remote? Ah. There on the coffee table. He clicked the button, settled back, propped up his feet and watched as panels on the far wall slid back, revealing a theater-sized flat-screen that was even sweeter than the one at his place. A quick check of the DVR revealed a *Doctor Who* marathon, along with *Night of the Living Dead* and—no effing way— *The Thing,* two of his all-time favorites.

He was overwhelmed by an unexpected feeling of…what? Not pleasure, because Gloria was upset. Contentment? Rightness? Belonging?

He couldn't name it.

All he knew was that he liked it, and her, and he liked her better the more he learned about her.

Prompted by his rumbling stomach, he pulled out his phone and dialed Bruce, who was no doubt circling the block or idling at the curb, awaiting further instructions.

Half an hour later, he was finishing off his third slice of pizza and about to select a fourth when a startled voice behind him made him jump out of his skin.

"Oh, my God! What the hell are you still doing here?"

He leaped to his feet and wheeled around to face Gloria, who was gaping at him.

"Eating pizza," he told her around a large mouthful.

"Why?" she cried.

"I was hungry."

"No! Why are you still here?"

"You were upset," he said simply.

She stared at him.

"Oh," she said faintly.

He waited for her verdict, his throat tight and his mouth dry.

"Just my luck," she muttered after several long beats. "Trapped in my own apartment with a crazy-ass Boy Scout."

"Eagle Scout. Just to clarify." He worked hard to keep his relief on lockdown and show some level of contrition. He knew he'd had no business hanging out. Well…no business other than his growing fascination with her. "And I'm sorry. If I took advantage."

She snorted. *"If?"*

He pressed his lips together to keep them from twitching. "I did provide the food."

"And you ate the food," she snapped.

"I saved you some."

Still fuming, she jammed a hand on her hip and divided her glare between him, the pizza box and his glass of pomegranate juice on the coffee table.

"I used a coaster," he pointed out.

A hint of amusement lit her expression for the first time as she looked to the TV. *"Doctor Who?"*

He grinned. "You have good taste in recorded shows."

That seemed to mollify her a little. She considered the pizza again, taking her time about deciding his fate. He used the opportunity to consider her.

Just showered fresh, fragrant with floral body wash or lotion or God-knew-what, she was a dizzying temptation. The most challenging possible test of his self-control.

The slinky black dress was gone, replaced by what was apparently her bedtime outfit, which consisted of a lacy white camisole shirt and a pair of white bikinis.

That was it.

Which meant that the gentle swells of her breasts were clearly visible, treating him to the sight of perfect dark nipples perfectly centered in breasts that would be, he was sure, perfect handfuls for him—

"You're not staring at my boobs, are you, Cooper?" she asked, now leaning over the coffee table to grab a napkin.

Caught, he decided to just roll with it.

"Nah. I've moved on to your ass."

And what an ass it was, high and round, tight with the kind of muscle definition that announced she was either a jogger or a dancer, possibly both. She didn't have much in the way of hips, but who the hell cared when her legs were long and shapely, without an ounce of fat on them?

Having selected a piece of pizza and put it on her plate, she turned to face him. Her face was washed and makeup-free, he realized, but she was, if anything, more beautiful without it, especially with that wicked gleam in her eyes.

"I never miss yoga class."

Yoga! God, he loved yoga.

"And I'm a runner, so I have a great body," she announced. "You probably noticed."

The understatement of the millennium right there. "Yes, ma'am. I noticed."

"And you're probably regretting not taking me up on my offer earlier, aren't you?"

"Yes, ma'am."

"Poor Cooper," she said. "That's a real shame, isn't it?"

"Truer words were never spoken," he agreed sourly.

"Because we'd be in my bed right now, wrapped around each other, and I'd be making you come until your eyes crossed."

He stilled, arrested by the images now cartwheeling through his overheated imagination, which included Gloria sweat-slicked and moaning as she arched beneath him, and his blood and face grew several degrees warmer. The front of his pants, meanwhile, was getting tighter by the second.

She was good, this one. She was very, very good.

But so was he.

"And you'd be saying my name." Raising his juice glass, he toasted her and sipped, holding her turbulent eyes as he did so. "Over and over again."

Gloria hesitated, her discreet gaze flickering to his crotch and back up again so quickly he would've missed it if he hadn't been so intensely focused on her.

"But now you have to lie in that horrible bed you made for yourself, don't you?" There was a new huskiness in her voice. "Pun intended."

He sighed. His hips, acting on their own accord, shifted restlessly. "Yes, ma'am."

"So keep your eyes in your head, okay?" she finished sweetly.

"I'll try. No promises. Can I stay?"

He waited, hoping that last question didn't sound too desperate and fearing that it did. Not that there was anything he could do about it, because he was quickly discovering that when it came to Gloria, he had precious little control over himself. And he really didn't want to be banished to his lonely apartment.

Not now that he knew what it was like to spend time here with her.

"That depends," she told him, dimpling. "Are there anchovies on this pizza?"

He blinked at her, trying to keep a handle on his soaring hopes. "Why would anyone order a pizza without anchovies?"

Grinning, she swept her hand toward the sofa, grabbed a fuzzy sweater off the end and slipped it on, covering herself enough for him to keep his sanity, then plopped to the right of where he'd been sitting. "Make yourself comfy."

Returning the grin, he sighed and collapsed back into his seat. This time he had no problem identifying the emotion welling inside him.

It was happiness.

The feeling was so overwhelming and delicious that he opened his mouth and spoke without thinking. "A man could seriously fall in love with you, Gloria."

The words landed hard, thudding into their new-found accord and mushrooming into a painful silence. Both of them hastily looked away, flushing and determined not to meet the other's eyes.

Chapter 4

They settled in and ate and watched *Doctor Who* without talking. Since he was a guy who could easily make a thousand words last several days, and since he was determined to take his cues from her and she seemed comfortable with the silence, it took him a while to notice that she wasn't laughing when he was…that she was just picking at her pizza…that— he shot her a sidelong glance—her expression was glazed and vacant as the ending credits rolled.

He checked his watch. It was half past dead of night. Time for him to go home.

Except that there was nothing waiting for him at home. Everything he wanted was here.

"Hey," he said quietly, nudging her shoulder as he clicked off the TV. "You okay?"

Startled out of whatever dark thoughts she'd been thinking, she nodded quickly—too quickly—ducked her head, swiped at her eyes and tried to smile.

"Yep. I'm not a fan of the Silence, though," she said, referring to the creatures in the episode they'd just watched. "Those things get on my nerves."

"I love the Silence."

"Well. You're a little strange, Eagle Scout. I think we've figured that out already." Her half smile, having never really caught on, faded away. To her credit, though, she seemed determined to overcome her moodiness. "Why'd you turn it off, though? There's another episode."

He took a quick inventory of her features, noting the smudges like bruises under her eyes, the red tip of her nose and the way she kept her lips pressed together, as though a sob was lingering on the other side of her teeth, waiting for the right moment to erupt. Deciding to risk it, he cupped her face, smoothing the fine silk of her temple with his thumb. She melted, just a little, letting her eyes drift closed and leaning into his touch.

"You need some sleep," he gently told her. "I should go."

Her lids flicked open, giving him another flash of the biggest, most spectacular brown eyes he'd ever seen.

Sad eyes.

"I won't be able to sleep tonight." She hesitated. "And I don't want to be alone."

He froze, not certain where she was going with this

and positive he didn't have the strength to stick to the moral high ground if she offered herself to him again. Not when this simple touch between them was causing his pulse to thump and desire to coil into a tight knot low in his belly.

"Gloria," he began.

"Please."

That was it for him. He nodded, easing back against the cushions again, his nerves strung like piano wire. What was the protocol here? Did she want to watch more TV? Eat more pizza? Apparently she felt as edgy as he did, because she leaped to her feet and looked around as though she'd forgotten something.

"I'm a terrible host," she said, looking toward the kitchen. "I didn't offer you a drink. I've got a really nice Cabernet, in case you like red—"

"I'm fine."

"—or some bourbon. You probably want bourbon, don't you?"

He reached out and grabbed her wrist, stopping her before she got more agitated. Her body felt as tight as his, and he felt the flex and play of the muscles in her arm as he hung on to her.

"Sit down," he urged. "Tell me."

She cast one longing glance into the kitchen, as though she wanted to sprint in there and hide in the cabinets, but then she surprised him by plopping back down beside him.

She hesitated, and then, "You're not judgy, are you?"

The answer came automatically.

"Me? Judgy? No way." He paused, deciding he'd better come clean. "What's *judgy?*"

Gloria scowled. "My sister is always judging me. It's this look she gets on her face—this pained look, like she's forcing herself not to tell me what an idiot I am. Everything is so black-and-white to her, and if I'm confused or—"

"I won't judge you, Doc," he said.

"Don't call me Doc."

"Sure thing, Doc."

She grinned. Her shoulders lost some of their rigidity as she leaned back beside him, tucking one foot under herself as she faced him.

"Tell me," he urged. "I won't think less of you."

She grimaced, giving him a hard stare. "Save it until you've heard how stupid I am."

This seemed to be a running theme with her, and he'd had enough of it. "You're not stupid, Gloria. Stop saying that."

"I've been having an affair with a married man." She hesitated. "One of the other docs at the hospital. He was separated from his wife when we hooked up, and I wasn't smart enough to cut him loose when they got back together. Or smart enough to know he was bullshitting me every time he said he planned to leave her again."

Cooper felt sick. He'd suspected as much, but the news still hit him like a swift jab to the Adam's apple, and he wasn't sure he could hide it. Not because of any particular moral outrage but because this was confirmation that she had a serious and long-standing emotional attachment to some punk who clearly didn't deserve her.

Nodding encouragingly, he tried to stifle his overwhelming urge to smash something. "Go on."

"I'm thirty-eight, Cooper."

Another nod.

"Which means," she said, her voice rising, "that not only am I way past old enough to know better, but I've wasted two good childbearing years—and I only have a few left!—waiting for that man to leave his wife for me!" Her lips twisted around a bitter laugh. "And guess what—it was all worth it! This whole time I've been waiting and waiting, and he's been promising and promising me, and my sister has been warning and judging me, over and over again like some endless loop from *Groundhog Day,* and today, finally, he told his wife he wanted a divorce!"

Shit, Cooper thought violently, his stomach lurching.

"Only guess what," she continued, voice cracking. "Karma's a bitch, Cooper, because he's leaving his wife, yeah, but he didn't leave her to be with me! He left her so he could 'find himself'!" She made quotation marks with her fingers. "And you know what that means, don't you? Say it with me—he can't commit to me, because he wants to be free to see other people! So it looks like I got what I deserved, doesn't it? And you know what that is. Say it with me—nothing! I get nothing. And that's exactly what I deserve."

With a final despairing look, she dropped her head and dabbed at her eyes with the corner of her sweater.

Which was great because it gave him time to school his features and think of something comforting to say. Plus he had plenty of questions about the whys and hows and whether she ever planned to see the cheating SOB again. But in all of this information, there was only one thing he had to know.

"You love him?" he asked dully.

She stilled. After a beat or two, she raised her head and stared off in the distance with unfocused eyes and a thoughtful frown. Words seemed to be on the tip of her tongue, but she didn't—couldn't?—say them.

"It's an easy question," he prompted.

"No." She shook her head. "It's not."

"Enlighten me."

Another pause. "Tonight, when I spoke to him before the gala, and he told me about his plans? I wanted to kill him."

That made two of them, Cooper thought angrily.

"And that's still what I feel. Rage. Because of all the time, emotions, hopes and dreams I wasted on that fool. And for what? He never met me halfway. He's never bothered to come here. He's never wanted to meet my sister. And why did I expect him to? I mean…seriously. What was I thinking? It's not like I knew he was a winning candidate from the get-go! And what did I even want from him? A real home? I have a real home! I bought it for myself." She gestured at her beautiful apartment. "Children? His children are almost grown now, and he told me a million times he didn't want any more. A loving and faithful partner?" She snorted. "He damn sure wasn't the one for that, was he, Cooper?"

He didn't answer.

"But the thing I'm most pissed off about is how I've felt about myself this whole time."

"What do you mean?"

She shrank inside her skin, head dipping so she didn't have to meet his eyes. Even her voice, when she spoke again, was smaller.

"I'm so ashamed of myself. I didn't think I was this woman. I've seen his wife at holiday parties and stuff. She looked like a nice person! I didn't think I could—"

She broke off on a stifled sob, shaking her head.

He sat in silence, giving her a minute.

"How did I land myself in this mess?" she finally asked, sounding stronger. "Why did I do it? To win? Because I couldn't stand the idea that another woman had something I didn't have?"

"Because you loved him?" Cooper asked, bringing it up again because she still hadn't given him a satisfactory answer and he needed to know, one way or the other. It felt as if his entire soul was tied up, being held hostage to her response.

"Why would I love someone like that?" There was an open curiosity in her eyes now, as though she sincerely hoped that Cooper—or someone—could explain the situation to her. "He's a liar and a cheater. He's selfish. And this whole two years, I haven't had a moment's peace. Between wondering when he'd call or show up, wondering why he hadn't, wondering when he'd ask his wife for a divorce, wondering if he'd had other affairs or if he was being a little too friendly with some of the nurses…it's just…I'm exhausted. I don't have anything left for this. I'm done with him."

Even though Cooper knew better than to bank on anything a person said in the heat of a breakup, especially after a long-term relationship, even if it'd been a dysfunctional one, his breathing began to ease up and his mood began to lighten. His heart, which had been thudding this whole time, began an excited tap dance. Still, he tried to rein himself in.

"Done?" he echoed dubiously. "It takes a while to unravel a relationship."

"I know." Her expression was direct. Honest. And, as far as he could tell, rage-free. "But when I think of all the damage this affair has done—" She broke off, shrugging helplessly. "Talia always says I'm my own worst enemy, and she's right. Why am I so self-destructive? Why would I put this much effort into something so toxic? Why didn't I just develop a drug habit and be done with it?"

There was an alarming image. "Don't say that."

"The only good thing about this whole mess is that his wife never knew. And I'll never tell her."

"Good," he said after a pause. "What else?"

She scrunched up her face, thinking hard before shooting him a wry smile. "I didn't mean to throw this all at you, Eagle Scout. You probably didn't think you'd be playing Dr. Phil when you offered to bring me home, did you? And you didn't even get laid for your trouble."

"Don't apologize," he said quickly. "You don't ever need to apologize to me."

"You're a good listener."

That made him laugh.

"What's so funny?"

"No one's ever accused me of that before. I was just thinking of the last several dozen women I've dated. They all complained about me checking my email or watching TV when they were trying to talk."

"You?"

"Me."

They grinned at each other and he felt that pleasant kick of adrenaline again—the thrilling burn of anticipation and excitement.

Maybe she felt it, too, because she suddenly looked away and became all business. "Well. Thanks for listening."

He watched her, worried she was about to kick him out. "Anytime, Doc."

Her expression clouded again, becoming raw. Vulnerable.

"I was right, though, wasn't I? Stoo-pid. That's me. Admit it."

"No," he said sharply, frowning. "I think you went into something that turned out to be a mistake. And now you're reevaluating. Seems pretty smart to me."

A tiny smile.

"And if it makes you feel any better," he added,

"you're not the only one who's ever hooked up with a married person. Trust me."

Her eyes widened. "Have you—?"

"Yeah. Nothing long-term, and I'm not proud of it, but—yeah. In my stupid younger days, I figured that if a man couldn't keep his wife satisfied, then she was fair game."

"So you're smarter now?"

"I hope so. Mama always quotes Maya Angelou at me. 'When you know better, you do better.'" He shrugged. "I figure you and I both know better now."

"I hope so. And that's enough about me for the night. I want to know how you and Marcus became brothers."

That made him laugh. "How we became brothers? Translation—what're you doing in a black family, white boy?"

"Well...yeah," she said, grinning.

He opened his mouth to tell her, and as always, the suffocating loss pressed in on him. It seemed more acute tonight, probably because it was late and he'd been drinking. Gloria's sharp eyes widened with concern, picking up on his emotion immediately.

"Sorry," she said quickly. "That was way too nosy, wasn't it?"

"Nope," he said, pressing his lips together before his chin began that embarrassing quivery thing it liked to do whenever he got upset. "You can ask me anything." He paused, breathing deep. "My birth dad died in a car accident before I was born. When I was ten, my mother was diagnosed with cancer. They gave her six months. There was no other family to take care of me, so she reached out to her best friend from college—Marlene Davies."

"Marcus's mom?"

"Yeah. I call her Mama. She came down to Atlanta to take care of Mom at the end. And me. Then she brought me up north, and suddenly I had a Pops and a knucklehead brother my age. They eventually adopted me, and the rest is history."

Gloria beamed at him, looking teary again but in a good way. "That's a great story. I needed a great story tonight. I'm glad you told me."

He stared at her, his hands itching to touch her face…to smooth her sleek cheeks…to stroke her full lips. "So am I."

The moment intensified between them, swelling until it felt as though there was nothing else in the apartment but this woman and his desire for her. And because he was so focused on her, he noticed the rosy flush that crept up from her neck and across her cheeks, the way her brown eyes brightened until they looked feverish, and the way her lids began to drift closed.

His body, acting on its own, began to lean in, reaching for her even though he'd sworn he wouldn't. "Gloria…"

The huskiness in his voice seemed to jar her back to her senses, which was good because he didn't seem to have any senses left.

Her breath hitched and she blinked, unfolding from the sofa and easing to her feet in one smooth move that would have fooled him if she hadn't been so pointed about keeping her gaze lowered so he couldn't see her expression.

He'd known it before, but now he felt it in a penetrating wave of heat that reached the marrow of his bones: Gloria wanted him physically, which was great—spectacular, really—but there was something more between them, and he wasn't alone in feeling that way.

"It's crazy late." Still not looking at him, she wrapped the edges of her sweater tighter around her middle and crossed her arms over her chest. But if they were defensive moves designed to defuse this moment between them, they failed miserably. All he could think about was the amazing body underneath her sweater. "I should let you get some sleep. I mean— you're staying, right? On the sofa, I mean? But not if you don't—"

"I'm staying."

"You are?" She met his gaze again, brightening as she pointed to a door off the hallway. "That's the powder room, and I've got extra toothbrushes and toothpaste under the sink, so help yourself."

"Great."

"And I'll bring you an extra blanket and pillow."

"Don't go to any trouble—"

But she was already gone, hurrying out of sight.

By the time he got back from brushing his teeth, she'd deposited a blanket and pillow on the end portion of the sectional and disappeared again. She'd probably gone to bed already, he thought, deflating a little. She was probably slipping into her big bed down the hall, her long limbs sliding against the cool sheets. Maybe she even peeled herself out of those little undies she'd been wearing and slept in the nude, those dark nipples pebbling and sensitive against Egyptian-cotton sheets—or maybe even satin sheets.

A man could dream, right?

And maybe tonight she'd even touch herself and think of him, he thought as he shrugged out of his dress shirt and swept his white undershirt over his head. Maybe she'd spread her thighs and rub her fingers... Hang on. Was she bare down there or not? He hoped she had a full bush, and since it was his fantasy, he was going to roll with that.

He unzipped the tightening crotch of his pants and kicked them off, toeing his way out of his socks as he did so. Maybe she'd also squeeze her nipples and arch her back, moaning. And what would she moan? Why, his name, of course. She'd cup and squeeze her breasts, pushing them together, and if he were there with her, he'd dip his head down and lick them before sucking an engorged nipple deep into his mouth. Maybe he'd scrape her gently with his teeth and see how she liked that.

She'd like it a lot, he was guessing.

Taking the blanket, he flapped it open to cover the sofa. Then he fluffed up his pillow and threw it back down, his surging testosterone making him rougher than he needed to be.

And then he'd run his tongue down her torso, he decided, the images flickering through his mind in high def, making sure to dip it into her belly button on his way south. Then, when he'd slid low enough, he'd nudge her hand aside and claim that sweet spot between her legs for his own. He'd wedge his shoulders between her thighs, opening her wider so he could see what he was doing, and then he'd lower his head to taste—

"Here's another pillow in case you— *Oh.*"

Gloria had arrived on her silent cat feet, startling him.

Her powers of speech sputtered and died when she saw what his right hand was doing:

Stroking over a rock-hard erection.

Embarrassment sent his face up in flames. With a muttered curse, he snatched up the pillow he'd just fluffed and used it to cover himself from her drop-jawed and wide-eyed gaze. The woman really needed to be outfitted with a bell so she'd quit scaring people to death, he thought sourly, waiting for her to say something, because he sure as hell didn't have anything on tap.

But she stared at his now-hidden crotch for several additional beats while her face went from red to purple. Only when she gasped and blinked, quickly looking away, did he realize that she'd been holding her breath.

One of her flustered hands went to her forehead and then fluttered through her hair. "I was just—"

By now his brain had fired up again. He opened his mouth to apologize, lest she think he was a pervert and call building security, but that wasn't what came out.

"Yeah, okay," he said, dropping the pillow with a flourish and opening his arms wide so she could see him in all his fully aroused, boxer-brief-clad glory. "I want you. You already know that. I'm not apologizing for it."

Her head came back around. She made a valiant effort to keep her attention on his face, but her overbright gaze dropped to his boner again, lingered for a heartbeat, then flickered back up to his eyes.

"You're masturbating."

No reason not to own it, since it was already laid out there on a silver platter.

"Yep."

"In my living room."

"Yep."

"And you're thinking of me while you're doing it."

"Yep. And just so you know—it's not the first time. *And* I've had dreams about you."

"Oh, my God."

"I just want all my cards out on the table."

"All of you seems to be out on the table."

He shrugged unapologetically, sweeping his arms wide again. "Deal with it."

"I wanted to deal with it!" she cried. "We could've been in my bedroom dealing with it—" she pointed at his erection "—right now! And you turned me down!"

Planting his feet wide and putting his hands on his hips, he squared off with her, leaning down in her face with as much dignity as possible under the circumstances.

"What's your point, Gloria?"

"What's my point?" She was aghast. "My point is that I don't get you, Cooper! What kind of man are you?"

That was easy.

"I'm the kind of man who's the opposite of the loser who's been wasting your time for the last couple of years," he told her quietly. She went still. "I'm the kind of man who wants more from you than one night of sex. In fact, I'm the kind of man who wants more than sex from you, and I'm willing to wait until the time is right for you, even if that's physically uncomfortable for me. Any other questions?"

Her gaze, searching and intent, never left his as she slowly shook her head.

"Great." He sprawled onto the sofa, flapped the blanket open over him and smashed the pillow into place beneath his head. "I'm beat."

Stretching his arm overhead, he reached for the end-table lamp and clicked it off, throwing her bewildered face into shadow. Then he rolled over, turning his back on her, and tried to settle in for what was sure to be a long and torturous night.

It turned out that leather, even the fine Italian leather of Gloria's sectionals, was not a good sleeping surface, especially when one was overheated, aroused and wakeful. Kicking off the blanket, which was, at this point, tangled by his feet anyway, Cooper rolled back to his stomach and let his arm dangle over the sofa's edge. But this position wasn't any better than the last four hundred positions he'd tried.

He sighed.

Checked his watch's lighted display: three-nineteen.

Sighed again.

Stared blearily at the city's lights, which were blurred on the other side of her sheer drapes.

Thrust his hips once or twice against the firm cushions, desperate for any relief his blue balls could get.

That was when he heard her again.

Without moving, he shifted his gaze from the windows to the hallway, his whole body focused on the soft padding of her bare feet as she approached. A second later, she materialized out of the darkness, a siren in only her shirt and panties. The blue-white from the moon's glow and the city's ambient light distinguished her from the shadows.

This was the third time she'd come.

She hovered on the living room's threshold. As he had the other two times, he waited, his body coiled tight, to see what she would do. What if her desire for him had blossomed to the point that she came closer, all the way to him? If so, would she touch him? What would he do if she did? Or would she quickly turn and slink back to her bedroom and close the door behind her, as she had the other two times?

The seconds marched on, marked by the faint ticking of his watch.

She stood there, motionless and watchful.

He couldn't take it anymore.

"Gloria." His voice was low and throaty with desire. "Go to bed."

"Come with me."

Her voice was sweet. Musical. Needy.

It swept over him, elusive and soft enough to make nerve endings tingle up his arms, across his shoulders and neck, and up into his scalp, forcing him to stifle a full-bodied groan.

Jesus. She was killing him, but he was not going to do this the easy way. Gloria was too important for that. He was going to do it the right way.

"No." Rolling back over, he levered up to sitting, making the leather creak, and reached out to her. "Come here."

He had one quick second to shore up his will, and then she was hurrying to him at a pace that was just this side of a run. She kept coming straight into his arms, and that was when the weakness got him. He half rose to catch her as she settled into a straddle on his lap, her knees resting on either side of his hips. He meant to hold her back a little, to say *whoa* and slow this train down before the inevitable crash, but touching her—feeling the solid warmth of her beneath his hands—was too intoxicating to refuse.

It was just for one minute, he told himself, even though he knew it was a lie. One minute wouldn't do any harm.

She stared straight into his face, her eyes glittering with hot excitement as she scraped her nails over his scalp and caught handfuls of hair at his nape. He watched her, dying to see what she would do…how far she would go if he let her…how wild an unleashed Gloria would be when he touched her.

And he wasn't an innocent party, despite his best

intentions. Not at all. His roving hands made their way up and down her silky thighs and around to her tight ass, cupping and kneading her so that the sweet spot between her thighs rubbed against his erection until he couldn't take it anymore. He wondered if it was possible to hyperventilate with pleasure, because God knew he couldn't regulate his breathing. And when she leaned her face down, he tipped his chin up, wallowing in the minty sweetness of her breath as she moved her mouth closer to his.

For one moment out of time it was all good: the crooning noises she made…the way he ran his hands up her sides, brushing his thumbs over her pebbled nipples…the way she arched her back to thrust her small breasts into his palms, filling them with her soft flesh…but when her lips came closer and her kiss was less than a whisper away, everything was, suddenly, all wrong.

A nightmare image of her in the morning filled his mind. He imagined her turning her face away from him and spouting the standard lines about how she'd made a mistake and wasn't ready for a relationship because she had loose ends with the punk who'd hurt her—he refused to entertain the thought that the other man might have broken her heart. That gave him just the zap of ice water to the veins that he needed to make sure common sense prevailed.

Cooper knew himself well enough to know that while resisting Gloria tonight might be painful, waking up to her cold shoulder after he'd spent time inside her delicious body—kissing her, loving her—would be excruciating.

So in the instant before their lips came together, he cupped either side of her face and held her still.

"I told you we're not doing this," he said sharply.

Gloria, to her credit, did not give up without a fight. Jerking her head free, she smiled a sultry woman's smile and diverted her mouth to the side of his neck so she could scrape him with her teeth while he moaned with exquisite pleasure.

"We *are* doing this," she murmured in his ear.

"No, we're not."

Galvanized by a wave of frustration, he acted quickly, before his overheated hormones influenced him any further. He grabbed her by the shoulders and pushed her back and off him, ignoring her shocked cry of protest. There was a struggle, but he was bigger and stronger, even though she did have his balls in a tight metaphorical grip. When it was all said and done, they were stretched out and spooning together, her back to his front, and his back against the cushions.

She was none too happy about her sudden loss of control, and she didn't play fair.

"Cooper." She whispered to him, circling her hips and grinding that perfect ass against his erection. "I'm so hot right now—"

"You don't say," he muttered.

"—and I need you." She writhed in his arms, cranking him higher. "Please, Cooper."

"Do you want me to leave?"

"What? *No.*"

"Then settle down so I can take care of you."

Those were apparently the magic words. She stilled and went quiet, until the harsh rasp of their breath was the only sound left in the world.

Certain now that he had her absolute attention, he went to work.

Dipping his face into the sweet hollow between her neck and shoulder—ah, man, she smelled like flowers and aroused woman, and she was seriously killing him—he bit, just hard enough, and was rewarded by her sharp cry of pleasure.

"You like that?" he asked, now running his tongue over the spot to soothe it.

"Yes."

"Are you thinking of him now?"

"No."

"I can't hear you."

"No."

He shifted behind her, rearranging his hands so that one was low on her taut belly and the other was flattened against her breast. He circled that hand, rubbing her hard nipple until her hips began to thrust involuntarily.

"What about now? Are you thinking of him now?"

"God, no," she breathed.

"Who are you thinking about?"

"You."

"And who am I? Say my name."

"Cooper."

"Again. So I can make sure you've got it."

"Cooper."

"Good girl." He'd thrown one leg over both of hers to keep her still a moment ago, but now he eased it off, freeing her. "Now I'll make you come."

"Please, Cooper. Please—"

"Spread your legs for me."

She was a model of compliance, melting into him with a sigh as she eased her thighs open in the hottest imaginable invitation. With another bite to her neck, he simultaneously ran the heel of his hand down her belly and over the silky panties that covered wiry hair beneath. Another shocked cry, and she began to move again, thrusting against him. His fingers itched to touch her bare flesh, knowing she'd be slick and petal soft, but he didn't think he could handle it without something snapping in his brain. He'd drawn a line in the sand and sworn he wouldn't cross it, and he meant it. There were things he knew better than to do, and touching her there, without panties between them, was one. Kissing her there was another. Kissing her perfect lips was a biggie.

But he could cool her off a little—oh, yes.

He could make her come until his touch was the only one she remembered.

So that was what he did, making tight, rhythmic circles with the heel of his hand as he zeroed in on her wet sex. Her breath stalled and hitched while her hips thrust against his hand, pumping harder and harder, until finally she let loose with a long, high cry, then went limp in his arms. And, feeling like the newly crowned emperor of the universe, he rubbed and stroked every part of her body he could reach, imprinting the feeling of her nipples…her hips and ass… her long legs on his mind forever, because he didn't know how long it'd be until he had her like this again.

And then she stirred, reaching a hand back and delving between his legs, where the mother of all erections still raged.

"Shhh," he told her, stopping her hand by grabbing and kissing it. "Go to sleep."

"But you—"

He grinned against her neck. "I've never been better. Trust me."

"Cooper," she said on a sexy, sated sigh. "Why are you here? Why are you doing this?"

Sliding his lips up to the delicate curve of her ear, he kept his voice low for a variety of reasons. Because the situation between them was evolving and fragile, and he didn't want to break it. Because he didn't want to scare her. Because he was already scared by how fast and how big this thing was, and saying it too loudly might make it even bigger.

But whispering was okay. He could whisper the truth to her.

"Because," he told her, "you're my woman. You just don't know it yet. Now go to sleep."

"Cooper," she repeated drowsily.

He strengthened his grip on her, anchoring her to him with a hand on her breast and the other on her sex, holding her tight so she'd know that she was far too precious to let go.

"Shhh," he repeated. "Go to sleep."

And without further protest, she did.

Chapter 5

Gloria woke to a ringing and a pounding, both of which seemed to be coming from inside her head.

"I'm up!" Long years of training as a medical student and resident kicked in, forcing her to bolt upright in bed. "I'm up. I'll be right there. Give me one second," she snapped, swinging one foot over the side so she could—

Whoa.

The room dipped and swerved around her. She pressed a hand to her head, wishing her brain would stop clanging inside her skull, and that was when the wave of nausea rolled up her throat, gaining momentum. Ah, shit. Hangover. Served her right for drinking like a college freshman last night, and champagne, too. Nothing was nastier the morning after than a bottle of champagne on the way back up.

But she drew the line at vomiting, which was disgusting beyond words. She was not going to barf—not on her bed or anywhere else, thanks. Scrambling to standing and hanging on to the furniture as she went, passing bed...nightstand...dresser...door frame...she made it into the bathroom, avoiding the mirrored medicine cabinet. There was no part of her that wanted to see what she looked like right now, but she wasn't taking any chances on an accidental glimpse. So she kept her lids closed, which had the added benefit of keeping the weak sunlight that was filtering through her blinds from stabbing her in the eyeballs. Reaching out, she fumbled around for her bin of essential oils and found it pretty quickly, which was great because bile had begun to collect around the dead rat she seemed to have in her mouth, and her tight throat had begun to spasm.

She would not throw up...she would *not*—

Moving too fast, she lost her grip on the bin and dropped it into the sink with a loud bang. The tiny bottles of essential oils clattered against the ceramic for what felt like ten agonizing minutes, each sound piercing her eardrums.

No. No, no, *no!* Where was the peppermint? She needed the peppermint— Oh, there it was!

Snatching it up, she unscrewed the lid, held it under her nose for a deep breath and—

Her throat spasmed again.

For a second or two, it could have gone either way. That revolting knot of bile hovered, refusing to go either up or down, until she breathed deep again. Swallowed hard. Used her free hand to hang on to the sink's edge for support. Suddenly, her stomach settled. She gasped in another deep breath, waiting.

The nausea eased up. It wasn't gone, but it was manageable.

Thank goodness.

That strange ringing, on the other hand, was still going.

What the hell was it?

After a quick rinse of mouthwash, she followed the sound back into her bedroom, where it seemed to be coming from the rumpled half of her bed. It was the fancy melodic ring of a cell phone, she realized, which was bizarre because she'd thrown her phone out the limo's window last night. She definitely remembered that. Maybe it was Cooper's phone, which would also be bizarre, because Cooper had not, to her knowledge, come into her bedroom last night, and there was no sign of him now.

Was he gone, then? Probably. Men didn't tend to stick around with her for long.

"Cooper?" Her voice was a broken rasp that wouldn't carry beyond the nightstand, so she cleared it and tried again. "Cooper? You here?"

No answer.

Her stomach, which had already seen a great deal of activity this morning, twinged with something that felt suspiciously like disappointment. That metallic ringing, meanwhile, continued. She tossed the pillows out of the way, looking for the source, and then saw the lighted display under the sheet. Aha!

Crawling across the bed and flipping the sheet aside, she revealed a cool-looking smartphone with a big screen. On it flashed a picture of Cooper that he'd obviously taken himself. The selfie showed him in all his blue-eyed, curly-haired, hard-jawed glory, looking incredibly sexy, as though he'd just climbed out of bed, with a prickly five-o'clock shadow across his chin and cheeks.

And if she needed any further clarification on who was calling, it was right there on the display.

Cooper, it said.

With a snort, she snapped the phone up and hit the green button.

"I would ask who this is," she said, "but you seem to have covered that."

"Oh, good." She could hear the laughter in his voice. "You found the phone."

"I found the phone. You're not in my kitchen, are you?"

"I'm home, getting ready for a flight to San Francisco in a couple of hours. I've got a meeting tomorrow, if you must know," he told her, and his smirk came through loud and clear. "Why? Did you miss me when you woke up?"

Her mind shifted, taking her back to their delicious moments on the sofa last night and the way his virtuoso hands had played her body. Flushing, she remembered drifting to sleep with him, wrapped up in his hard body with their legs intertwined. She thought of how relaxed she'd been. How content. And she looked at the smooth half of her bed, where the impression of his body would be now if he'd lain there with her. And she felt a sudden ache of loneliness inside.

She and loneliness, man. They were BFFs, weren't they?

"Why would I miss you?" she asked coolly.

"Right." Another laugh, this one with an edge of derisiveness, as though he'd hooked her up to some invisible truth detector and knew she was full of B.S. "I get it."

"Get what?" she snapped.

"I get *you,* Gloria," he said in a low murmur that sent a shiver—a delicious shiver—up her spine and across her scalp. "Did you get some sleep?"

"Yes," she admitted. Determined not to melt into a puddle of chocolate pudding, she rubbed her arms, trying to get rid of the unwanted goose bumps. "I don't remember getting in the bed, though."

"I tucked you in before I left."

"Tucked me in?" She thought of the five pounds—recently blossomed to seven—that she'd been trying to lose for the past, oh, fifteen years. "I have the gross tonnage of a newborn orca."

"No, you don't." His throaty laugh did nothing to help eradicate those goose bumps, and neither did the low seductive note in his voice. "And I'm hoping that me putting you in bed is the only thing you've forgotten about last night."

She remembered everything, alas. Every embarrassing, delicious and unexpected detail. His kindness…the intensity of his bright blue eyes, focused entirely on her…the way she'd thrown herself at him like the woman of questionable morals she clearly was…his chivalrous refusal to take her up on her semi-drunken offer to sleep with him…and, most disquieting of all, the way he'd refused to kiss her mouth even as his hands danced across her body like Horowitz playing a Steinway.

Oh, yes. She remembered.

But that didn't mean she had to admit it to him. She opened her mouth to issue a denial and discovered, too late, that it wouldn't come.

"I…" she said faintly.

Her voice trailed off, and that was more than answer enough.

The soft rasp of his breath was his only response. The silence between them intensified until her skin felt tight and her blood hot. Which was a disaster in the making, because her body shouldn't crave a new man—she shouldn't like a new man quite so much— just as she was coming to her senses about the old man. She had no intentions of repeating any of her past foolish choices.

"Cooper," she began, determined to put the brakes on this thing between them, whatever it was, "about what happened last night—"

"No explanations." His voice was firm. "No apologies. No regrets. Okay?"

"But—" Thrown for a loop, she tried to decide which would be worse: being let off the hook entirely when they probably needed to clear the air, or keeping the conversation going by arguing that all the champagne she'd drunk last night had lowered her inhibitions and made her into gooey caramel when he touched her. "I feel like we should—"

"We shouldn't. Trust me. So how do you like your new phone?"

Faltering at this abrupt change of topic, she blinked and tried to refocus.

"It—It's not my phone."

"It is now. Since you threw your old one out the window last night and you need a phone."

"I was planning to get a new phone. Today. When I woke up at a normal hour and not—" she checked her nightstand clock "—seven twenty-nine in the morning. *Sunday* morning."

"Maybe, but would you have given me your new number? I didn't want to take any chances."

"So you—what? Found some twenty-four-hour drive-through cell phone store? Unbelievable."

"Pretty much. Well, Bruce, the driver, did."

"Well, that's really nice of you." She pulled the phone back a little, looking wistfully at the huge bright screen, which was sleek and way nicer than her old phone's. "And it's a great phone, but I can't keep it."

"Why not? It's all set up in your name."

"It is?"

"Of course."

She frowned, determined to find a loophole in this offer and force him to reveal himself to be the jerk she knew had to be hiding in there somewhere. All men were jerks who wanted only one thing from women. The only variable was how well they hid it.

"I can't accept it. Cell phones are expensive."

"Yeah," he said drily. "That couple hundred bucks really set me back. I'll be eating canned chicken soup all month now. What will I do?"

She rolled her eyes, knowing damn well, as every New Yorker did, that the Davies family and their auction house did extremely well for themselves and could probably buy and sell half of Manhattan if they wanted to.

"I'll write you a check, smart-ass."

She could almost hear him shrug. "Suit yourself."

A troubling new thought hit her. "And did you put some sort of tracking or listening device in it?"

There was a long pause.

"And why would I do that?" he asked, a distinct chill in his voice now.

"What if you're a stalker or something?"

This seemed like a very reasonable concern for a single woman to have, even though she found herself fidgeting uncomfortably. Worse, prickly heat was inching up the sides of her face, as though her body knew she'd gone too far by being rude to a man who'd done her a favor, even if her stupid brain refused to acknowledge it.

There was a longer pause.

"If I was a stalker or something," he said finally, and she could practically hear the clink of ice cubes in his tone now, "I think we both know that I could've done you some serious damage last night." A beat or two went by. She squirmed. "But if you don't want the phone, I'm sure you'll think of a creative way to get rid of it. You're good at that. Garbage disposal, maybe?"

She laughed. "Eagle Scout rides again. Do you have a cape to go with your uniform?"

"I think you're getting the wrong idea about me." His voice was considerably warmer. "I'm no angel."

This simple statement killed her humor, especially when an image of Aaron flashed through her mind. "I would never think any man was an angel," she said flatly. "Trust me. But I really appreciate the phone. Thanks."

"Hmm." He seemed to detect that she was sliding into a dark mood, because he came up with a quick diversion. "So listen, the thing you need to remember is the three raw eggs and a full tablespoon of hot sauce. Got it?"

"Got it," she said, trying to rub away some of the headache that was currently pounding between her eyes.

"So." His tone was crisp now. Impersonal. "I'll let you go. I've got my flight."

"Oh. Okay. Yeah." She hesitated, trying to squash the unsettling swoop of disappointment in her belly. Was that it, then? Just like that? Was he going to hang up without trying to see her again? Without asking her what she planned to do about Aaron now that she'd slept on it? "Are you packed?"

"Almost."

"When will you be back?" She wanted to bite her tongue off as soon as the words were out of her mouth, but she'd developed an irritating and persistent desire to know more about him.

"I'm not sure," he said.

"Oh."

There was an awkward pause, which he did nothing to fill.

"Well." She pressed her lips together, rolled her eyes and shook her head at herself, glad he wasn't there to see her in all her waffling idiocy. "Travel safe."

"Thanks."

"Well," she said lightly, flopping over onto her back and taking her inexplicable frustration out on the mattress, which she thumped with her feet. "Bye."

"I'll be in touch, Doc."

This simple statement made her ears perk. She stopped thumping and abruptly sat up again, making the room swivel like an amusement park ride. What did that mean, he'd be in touch?

"You will?" she asked.

But the line was silent.

"Cooper? Hello?" she said, pulling the phone away from her ear to check the display, which was now blank.

Someone knocked on her front door, startling her. Luckily, it also stopped her from wondering whether she should call Cooper back. She hesitated. The knock sounded again, more insistent this time.

What the hell?

Since she wasn't dressed and the sun wasn't fully up yet, she was tempted to ignore it. Most likely someone had come to visit a neighbor and needed to take a closer look at the numbers on the doors. But then the knocking turned into the kind of frantic pounding that signaled a fire or some other disaster, so she grabbed her robe from the end of the bed, yanked it on and hurried out into the hallway, where she heard a muffled voice calling her name.

That wasn't her sister, Talia, was it?

She'd made it across the living room and was almost in the foyer when the lock clicked, the door swung open, and Talia and the building manager, both looking wild-eyed, tumbled into her apartment.

"Gloria!" Talia cried.

"What the hell are you doing?" Gloria snapped, glaring at them both as she jerkily tied her robe's belt. "It's a quarter before dawn!"

"We thought you were dead!" Talia snapped back, now looking outraged. "I had to wake up Roy and ask him to break in to make sure Cooper hadn't abducted you or you weren't dead of a heart attack on your bathroom floor or something! Why haven't you answered your phone all night?"

"Um…" Gloria tried not to fidget or look shifty. "It's, ah, broken."

"Broken?"

"That's what I said." Gloria realized she was ruffling her hair and forced herself to drop her hand. *"Broken."*

"Well, what's that in your hand, then?"

Gloria frowned and dropped her replacement phone into her robe pocket. "I'll tell you later." She shifted her attention to the building manager, who was now yawning and withdrawing his master key from her lock. "Sorry, Roy."

"Always glad to help, Dr. Adams." With another yawn, he left.

This gave Gloria the opportunity to focus on Talia, who didn't look too good as they headed for the living room. Which begged the question: Why had Talia been looking for her this early? After last night's triumphant unveiling of her mural at the auction house, Talia should have gone home and spent the night being chased around the bed by her boyfriend, Tony Davies. Not showing up here with ashen skin, hollowed-out eyes and the haunted expression Gloria remembered all too well from traumas past.

She stilled, the words stalling in her tight throat because she didn't want to ask the question. She opened her mouth, then shut it. Cleared her throat and tried again, sinking onto the edge of the sofa as she did so.

"You're scaring me, Tally. What's wrong? Why were you looking for me?"

"I think it's back." Tally's face twisted. She sat on the ottoman opposite Gloria and looked up at the ceiling. Muscles contracted in her throat, as though she was trying either to force the words out or to swallow them back. Ducking her head, she wiped her eyes and stared at Gloria, her expression bleak. "Actually, that's not true. I don't *think*." She took a shuddering breath. "It's back."

Gloria stared at her, mute and uncomprehending, even though there was only one thing that had ever made Talia look that lost. Not even the death of their father, who'd left the family for his secretary when they were teenagers and then died of cardiac arrest in his other girlfriend's bed two years later, or the lung cancer death of their mother three years after that had made Talia look so forlorn.

No, there was only one thing that struck this kind of fear in their hearts, only one *it*.

Talia's Hodgkin's disease was back.

"Oh," Gloria said faintly, twining her fingers in her lap to keep her hands from shaking. "Okay."

"I'm going to the doctor Monday. First thing."

Gloria nodded, grateful for the numbness that was setting in. "Okay."

"Will you come with me?"

"Of course."

"Good." Talia looked relieved. "You can explain the medical jargon to me in plain English."

Gloria kept quiet on that one. She'd long ago realized that that was the ironic thing about her medical license: it was worthless when it came to her baby sister, the only living relative she had left. Talia was the most important person in her life, and when her life was threatened, Gloria wasn't an M.D. She couldn't think rationally. She couldn't interpret test results and blood counts, and she damn sure couldn't discuss prognoses and likelihoods. She was just a scared little girl in need of a dark closet where she could sob her eyes out.

And to think that ten minutes ago, her biggest worries had been Cooper and Aaron. That was the sad truth about cancer, she supposed: it put all of life's other nonsense into perspective.

"Did you tell Tony?"

Talia's stoicism seemed to waver, making her lips

twist and her nostrils flare. She nodded, blinking back tears.

"And?"

"He was angry with me for keeping it from him last night at the party." Talia brushed the back of her hand past her eyes and took a deep breath. "He'd been planning to ask me to marry him."

A bitter chill started in Gloria's gut and spread all the way to her fingertips. She didn't know Tony well, and she'd known a lot of rat bastards in her life, but Tony didn't seem to be one of them. She thought of the way she'd seen him look at Talia as though her gray eyes held all the secrets to the universe, and it just didn't add up.

"He didn't retract his proposal, did he?"

"No," Talia said quickly. "But I can't ask him to go through this with me."

This, like *it,* required no explanation. *This* encompassed the tests, the chemotherapy and the additional tests to make sure the chemotherapy was working. Not to mention the possible surgery and side effects. There were always side effects, and they were often painful and disgusting, and Gloria knew that Talia didn't want Tony to see her like that.

She probably also didn't want to test the strength of Tony's feelings for her this early in their relationship, because what if he failed? What if he couldn't take it when her hair fell out?

Gloria understood all of Talia's fears. But then she thought again of the way Tony looked at Talia, and she knew they were baseless.

"He loves you, Tally," she said quietly. "Don't push him away now. You're going to need him."

Talia didn't seem to know how to handle this information. A sound—half laugh, half sob—burst out of her throat. "I thought you suspected him of all kinds of nefarious motives!"

"All men are guilty of nefarious motives, Tally. Have I taught you nothing?"

Talia laughed weakly.

"But Tony's motives seem less nefarious than others'," Gloria assured her. "Which is why I've let him live." She thought about that. "Thus far."

Another halfhearted laugh from Talia, and then a lightbulb seemed to go off over her head. "I almost forgot. Speaking of the way men look at us—"

Uh-oh, Gloria thought.

"—what happened when Cooper brought you home last night? Anything?"

"Nope," Gloria said lightly, shrugging.

"You're such a liar! You always shrug when you lie!"

"Not true," Gloria said, fighting her shoulders' desire that very second to lift up to her ears. In the end, her right shoulder hitched up and she played it off by using it to scratch her earlobe. "Just an itch."

That broke up some of the tension. They grinned at each other and then, just as quickly, Talia's laughter turned to racking sobs.

"I'm so scared," she said, doubling up and curling in on herself. "I am so freaking scared."

Since they both couldn't be scared at the same time,

Gloria decided that this was her moment to be the strong one. There was always time later for her to fall apart in the shower.

"Come here."

Gloria opened her arms, and Talia scurried over to her side of the sofa and collapsed gratefully against her, sobbing. Together they settled in, getting comfortable as they assumed the positions they'd used so many times before, when they had only each other to rely on. Gloria put a pillow in her lap. Talia laid her head down and stretched out, her entire body shaking as she cried.

Gloria eased off Talia's wig—today's version was a black pixie cut that covered the downy wisps that had grown in since her first round of treatment—and ran her hand over her sister's overheated and damp forehead. Then she rubbed her shoulder and down her back before circling back up to her forehead and starting all over again.

The whole time, she shifted her knees back and forth, rocking Talia, and absently hummed "Danny Boy," the song their mother had always used on them when they needed comforting.

It took forever to settle Talia down. She quieted several times only to start back up again, as though she'd been stockpiling tears for just such an occasion. Or maybe Talia's sorrow was magnified because she was in love with Tony now and therefore had much more to lose.

Not that it mattered. Anyone facing a serious diagnosis deserved at least one good cry without someone muttering platitudes about how it was all going to be okay, so Gloria didn't say anything or try to shush her up. There'd be time for pep talks later.

Eventually, when the pillow was soaked and bright morning sun was filtering through the drapes, Talia's breathing evened out and her body relaxed. Gloria waited five more minutes just in case, but Talia was asleep.

Taking all the care in the world, Gloria eased sideways so that the pillow rested on the sofa rather than her lap. Then she stood and stared down at her sister, who was curled into a ball and looking as fragile as a newborn kitten. Gloria's heart contracted with a sudden pain so sharp it erupted in a choked sound. Clamping a hand over her mouth, she held it back even if she couldn't stop the tears that fell on Talia's body as she covered her with the throw.

Only when Talia was tucked in nice and safe, for now at least, did Gloria give herself permission to lose it. She raced out of the living room and down the hall toward her bedroom. It felt as though her sobs were chasing her because they came hard and hot, one after the other, and she had no more chance of outrunning them than she did of waving a magic wand and taking this burden away from Talia.

All either one of them could do was try to make it to the other side.

So she collapsed on her bed, buried her face in the pillow and gave herself five minutes—no more—to cry for Talia. And then she gave herself thirty angry seconds—no more—to kick herself for her past mistakes with Aaron and cry for the demise of the romantic relationship on which she'd pinned so many doomed hopes.

Chapter 6

That night, Gloria dipped her toe in her oversize bathtub, testing the water. Since it was just this side of scalding, sending a white-hot shot of heat straight up her body and out her brain, she decided it was perfect. As were the frothy mound of lavender bubble bath, the Marvin Gaye piping in through the speakers, the sensual relaxation candle burning on the counter and the tall-stemmed glass of Chardonnay with the single ice cube in it—tacky, yeah, but she liked her wine to stay chilled—that stood on the tub's ledge.

Sighing with relief that this long and stressful day and the dull thud of her hangover headache had finally dimmed once she followed Cooper's advice and drank that disgusting concoction, she slid into the tub. Wincing against the delicious heat, she reached for the sci-fi novel she'd been reading, leaned back against the terrycloth pillow and flipped open to her page.

Over on the counter, her phone rang.

She stiffened, cursing.

But then she remembered that the only person who had her new number was Cooper, and she felt an unsettling swoop of excitement. Without giving herself time for second thoughts, she half rose, grabbed the phone and sank back down, all with a great slosh of water.

She hit the button by the third ring, catching a quick glimpse of his face on the display.

"Hello?"

"San Francisco isn't a bad city," he said. "Agree or disagree?"

That made her grin for what felt like the first time in years.

"Disagree. I've been there for a couple conferences and a marathon. San Francisco is a *great* city."

"Wrong. San Francisco would have to consistently be twenty degrees warmer to be a great city."

"Well, I'm entitled to my opinion," she told him.

"Your opinion is wrong," he said flatly.

She laughed outright.

"And what was your marathon time, pray?"

"Four ten thirteen. Why?"

"That's not very good, is it? My time was three fifty-seven eleven."

"There were hills! My time was very good, thank you!"

"Ah, but mine was much better."

"Competitive much?"

"Yeah. Much."

"So you made it, I take it?" she asked, still laughing.

"I made it. Going to Chinatown for dinner in a few."

"Oh, I'm jealous."

"You should be. What're you doing? I hear water."

"I'm taking a bath."

Silence.

"Cooper?"

"I'm going to need a minute on that one."

"Come again?"

"A bath? So you're wearing what?"

Another laugh. "Nothing."

"Yeah, okay," he said, sighing harshly. "I'm going to need another minute."

"Why?"

"Why? Well, first I need to get all kinds of images of your naked body out of my head. Then I need to not ask you to send me a picture, and I definitely don't want to mention phone sex. That would be rude."

"Right," she murmured.

Although, to be honest, the idea of sliding her wet and slippery hands over her hard nipples and then between her thighs, all while listening to the low velvet of his voice, wasn't the worst one she'd ever had.

"Right," he echoed hoarsely.

They were both silent. Gloria pressed her thighs together, trying to keep her agitated body under control, causing the water to lap against the side of the tub.

She felt Cooper's interest sharpen over the phone. "What was that noise?"

"Nothing," she lied.

"Right." He heaved another sigh. "So how was your day?"

The thought of Talia put the kibosh on any sexy thoughts she'd been having, and her stomach sank. She hesitated, knowing how much Talia valued her privacy, and took a sip of wine.

"It was okay."

"*Okay?* There's a ringing endorsement. Did you take my hangover cure?"

"Yeah. I had to run out to get the eggs. But it worked. Thanks."

"So…did anything much happen to you today?"

The name Aaron hung in the air between them, but he didn't say it and for that she was grateful.

Talia's privacy was important, yeah, Gloria decided, but her cancer recurrence was happening to Gloria, too, and Gloria needed a friend she could talk to right now. And God knew Aaron had never, and would never, fit that bill.

"I can talk to you in confidence, can't I?"

"Everything you tell me is in confidence, Doc."

Taking a deep breath, she plowed ahead. "Talia's probably had a recurrence of Hodgkin's disease. She has an appointment tomorrow morning. I'm going with her."

The long silence told her he was stunned and probably had no idea Talia had ever battled cancer. She wasn't surprised. Talia was fierce about protecting her privacy and not wanting people to feel sorry for her.

"I'm sorry." His voice was heavy with sincerity. "Talia's good people. I like her a lot."

"Thanks," Gloria told him. "I appreciate that."

"Isn't this one of those things you shouldn't worry about until you know for sure? Won't there be lots of tests and—?"

"If it was anyone else, I'd say yes. But Talia's really in tune with her body. That's how they were able to catch it early when she was diagnosed—she kept insisting that something was wrong." She shrugged. "If she says it's back, it's back."

"Man," he said.

"I know. She doesn't deserve this."

"How's she doing?"

"She's tough. She's spending the night here."

"And how are you?"

The reply was automatic. "I'm fine."

"Doc." His voice felt like the gentlest possible caress across her face. "Don't. You don't have to with me."

With that, she opened her mouth, and the words were up and out before she could stop them.

"I can't lose my sister, too. Not. Talia."

He didn't say anything for a couple seconds, which gave her a chance to get her vehemence under control. Her whole body was trembling with it, causing water to slosh over the sides again.

"Your parents are gone?"

"Yeah. So it's up to me to take care of her."

"Then Talia's in the best possible hands."

"I'm not so sure about that," she said with a shaky laugh.

"I am."

His quiet confidence made her feel better.

Willing herself to relax, she leaned against the pillow again and let her eyes drift closed. "From your lips to God's ears, Eagle Scout."

He seemed to know her energy was waning. "So," he said. "I'll let you go. It's late there—"

"Not yet," she said quickly, then thought better of it. "I mean…sorry. You've got dinner and here I am talking your ear off."

"I have strong ears," he assured her. "And plenty of time for you."

Words felt as if they were on the tip of her tongue, but she had no hope of stringing them together. "I just… I hope you have a good trip. Get lots of business done. Make some money."

It sounded as though he was grinning. "Will do."

"Thanks for checking up on me, Cooper."

"Don't thank me," he said flatly.

"Why not?"

"Because talking to you and being there for you and becoming part of your life is all part of my plan."

She frowned, excruciatingly aware of her thudding pulse and the way sudden shivers were racing across her skin. "And what plan is that?"

"The plan to make you fall crazy in love with me. What else?"

With that stunning announcement still ringing in her ear, he hung up.

The next morning, Gloria checked her watch as she hurried down the windowed corridor to the coffee stand in her medical office building. Nine forty-seven, which was better than she'd hoped for. She'd just come from Talia's doctor's appointment, which had gone as quickly and smoothly as possible. And Tony had surprised Talia with a proposal before the appointment, which had been a wonderfully emotional moment.

She was thrilled that Talia was getting married. No one deserved happiness more than Talia did.

It was just that Talia's love story underscored Gloria's loneliness.

But she wasn't going to think about that now, much less dwell on it. She was too busy. The morning's events had left her with just enough time to grab some coffee and oatmeal and check in with her staff before she started her morning round of appointments at ten-ten. First up? A high school senior whose eighteenth birthday present was going to be a rhinoplasty to remove a microscopic bump on the ridge of her nose.

Frivolous compared to the life-or-death drama that Talia was currently enduring?

Oh, yeah.

Was it just what Gloria needed to normalize her day a little bit?

Damn straight.

"Hi, Fran." Waving at the barista behind the counter, Gloria fished a ten out of her lab coat pocket. "Can I have the usual? With hot milk? And maybe one of those bananas. No, the one next to it."

A man's figure materialized to her right. "Is that you, Dr. Adams?"

Gloria stiffened and nodded an unsmiling greeting. Accepting the empty paper cup from Fran with as much grace as she could muster, which was about half an ounce, Gloria moved to the side table and pumped some coffee from the huge thermos.

Making a production of adding cream and sweetener, Gloria kept her head low and tried to decide how she felt about being confronted by Aaron this early on a difficult Monday morning.

Not good. She had the same sort of "oh, shit" feeling sinking in the pit of her stomach that she had when she was speeding down the highway and saw the flash of police lights in her rearview mirror.

Which was a far cry from the tingly anticipation she'd felt over the past couple of years when there was the slightest chance of running into Aaron or even catching a glimpse of him. She realized in that very second that she'd be perfectly fine if she never laid eyes on him again.

In fact, she'd prefer it.

"Just a large coffee for me," Aaron said. "Thanks, Fran."

And then he was right there at Gloria's elbow again, a literal and figurative shadow over her. "Morning, Glo," he said low.

Caught, Gloria turned to face the man whose voice was as smooth and dark as his brown skin. He wasn't tall but he was cut, with a tailored lab coat that hit his broad shoulders just right, a dress shirt with French cuffs and gold-and-onyx cuff links, wool slacks and a pair of leather loafers that he'd bought during a family vacation in Italy last April. Which was why he'd missed—and forgotten—her thirty-eighth birthday, although, to be fair, he had made up for it by giving her a beautiful pair of diamond studs.

This was back when she'd been stupid enough to think that a swipe of his credit card equaled real emotional connection. Now she was smarter.

She looked into his face, deciding on the spot to sell the earrings and give the proceeds to a lymphoma charity. Maybe then the money could go to some good use, benefiting Talia and other cancer patients like her.

"Good morning," she said coolly, putting the lid on her coffee and throwing away the stirrer.

"Where've you been?" he asked urgently.

That was the thing about Aaron—his general irresistibility. On the checklist of what made a man hot, he had every box marked off: brown eyes that were hooded and penetrating; a straight nose; a chiseled jaw; a dimpled chin; full lips; a sexy voice; a faint musky scent of cologne; a dusting of gray hair through his temples that added an unmistakable air of wisdom and maturity; and, worst of all, a way of looking at her that made her feel like the only person in the world. The flip side of that particular trait, unfortunately, was that they weren't together that much, so he didn't spend much time looking at her.

Which meant she spent a huge amount of time feeling worthless to him or, worse, invisible.

Her future brother-in-law, Tony, meanwhile, spent a lot of time gazing at Talia as though he'd never seen anyone so miraculous. That was what Gloria wanted. What every woman wanted—to feel special. It wasn't too much to ask for.

So she was done wasting her time with *this*.

With him.

"Where've I been?" she echoed.

"Yeah," he said, easing closer. "I've been calling and texting you all weekend. Don't pretend you didn't know."

"I didn't, actually. I got a new phone."

"Yeah?" Reaching into his lab coat pocket, he produced his own phone and paused, his thumb poised over the screen. "What's the number?"

Gloria stared at him, honestly puzzled. "Why would you need it?"

"Dr. Adams?" Fran held out a bowl. "Here's your oatmeal."

Gloria smiled, took it and started on her way back to her office. "Thanks, Fran."

Aaron was hot on her heels. "Why would I need your number? Did you just ask me that?"

"Yeah," she said without breaking stride as they veered around a technician rolling a cart. "Since we agreed it's over, what else is there to say?"

Aaron put a heavy hand on her arm, stopping her.

His soulful eyes, now wounded, raw and vulnerable, had widened to fill up his entire face. "I didn't agree to anything like that. What's gotten into you, baby?"

Ah, there it was. The generic *baby,* which could fit whether he was in bed with his wife, with Gloria or with one of the other women he was probably sleeping with.

Mindful of another passerby and of the time, she carefully pulled her arm free and kept her voice quiet. Keeping her face blankly professional was harder. "You're getting a divorce. You want to see other people. Go see other people. Godspeed. Bye. I told you this already. What's the mystery?"

"We need to talk about this. I'm not giving you up."

She rolled her eyes at his husky urgency and started walking again. Now that she'd finally opened her eyes to his toxic mind games, man, they were really open. And he was a freaking grand master.

"Newsflash—I'm not yours to give up or to keep. Bye."

That hand clamped down on her arm again. His voice, meanwhile, pitched higher with unmistakable frustration. "Stop saying *bye.*"

For the first time since he'd approached her, she felt a flare of anger.

"Don't. Touch. Me."

Something in her expression must have told him she meant business—that he was about to lose a limb and it didn't matter if they were in a public place or not—because he withdrew his hand.

She turned the corner into the smaller corridor outside the back entrance to her office. Stacking the oatmeal on top of the coffee, she reached for her key card and swiped it.

"I don't have time for this. I have patients."

But Aaron was building up a head of steam and seemed determined to plead his tired case in its entirety. "You have to understand, baby. I've been married twenty years. I'm not in a position to marry you or anybody else—"

That was, possibly, the most ridiculous thing she'd ever heard. "Why would I want to marry you?" she said on a startled laugh. "So you could cheat on me?"

Aaron blinked at her, clearly as stupefied as if she'd started speaking Russian. Deciding that this was her chance, she turned the knob and ducked into the back hallway of her suite of offices. Hopefully he would take the hint and leave so she could eat in peace.

But he didn't leave.

He pushed through the door behind her.

Outraged, she opened her mouth, ready to rip him a new one, but Sandy, her office manager, came out of their kitchen at that precise moment. She'd been stirring a cup of yogurt, but now she looked up, dividing her speculative gaze between them.

Gloria smiled and tried to look casual even though her cheeks were now burning with embarrassment. Here was another reason to hate Aaron. He didn't want to be seen with her in any restaurant, theater, park or public place in Manhattan, but he had no problems slinking into the back door of her office and subjecting her to nosy stares like the one on Sandy's face.

If Sandy didn't suspect they were having an affair, then Gloria was the reincarnation of Marilyn Monroe.

"Morning, Sandy," Gloria said, wanting the floor to open up and swallow her whole before she could spend any more time wondering what her employees thought of her. The only good thing about this situation was that Sandy was discreet and loyal. "I've just got a quick consult with Dr. Madden before my first patient. Did I miss anything this morning?"

"Nope," Sandy assured her, continuing on her way to her desk. "Morning, Dr. Madden."

"How're you doing?" Aaron answered vaguely.

Gloria and Aaron filed into Gloria's office. She shut the door but didn't bother sitting. She was out of patience, and Aaron wasn't going to be here that long.

She got right up in his face.

"What?" she demanded. "You've got ten seconds."

To no one's surprise, Aaron launched a full-out charm offensive.

"You're hurt." Nodding like the soul of sensitivity, he dimpled at her, eased closer and reached for her waist. "I understand that—"

"Understand this," she said sweetly. "If you touch me again—ever—I will slap you. And I don't care who hears it."

His expression cooling by several degrees, he took a step back. "There's someone else, isn't there? You're screwing someone else, aren't you?"

This accusation, coming from him, was so incongruous—so patently outrageous—that the only thing she could do was laugh.

He bristled.

"Coming from the man who's been sleeping with a woman other than his wife for the last two years? Wow. That's rich."

"You think this is funny? I asked you a question, Glo."

"What I do is no longer any of your business," she said, standing firm as her amusement slipped away. "And you need to leave."

He didn't move.

They faced off in a brittle silence, with Gloria wondering where she'd finally gotten the courage to end it and mean it. Maybe it was as simple as God's light hand on her shoulder, giving her the strength to decide what was and wasn't okay with her and to settle for nothing less. In the end it didn't matter. The only thing that mattered was that this was over, and she meant it.

The funny thing was, she wasn't particularly angry or sad about it.

Just resolute.

Consternation formed such deep groove lines between his eyes that she almost felt sorry for him.

"You love me." The closest thing she'd ever seen to genuine pain flashed across his expression. "That doesn't end like that." He snapped his fingers. "This can't be over like that." Another snap.

She tilted her head and thought about it.

"I was attracted to you. I wanted you. I waited for you." She paused, wanting to get it all out there and to say it right, because she knew this chance wouldn't come again. "I gave everything I had to you. I threw away my moral code for you. I felt guilty for you. I hid in the shadows. For you."

He shook his head and raised a hand, clearly wanting to slow her down. "Gloria—"

"I put my life on hold for you. For two years. I thought I loved you. I thought we were worth it, but now—"

Hope lit his face as he reached out for her. "We are worth it, baby."

She shrugged helplessly. "But now I just look at you and see…a waste of time. A lesson learned." She pressed her lips together, trying not to let a sudden flare of bitterness get the best of her. "All I see is a man who doesn't care about what I need or want." She hesitated, then decided there was no point to pulling her punches now. "A selfish man."

He took an aggressive step forward, his heavy brows flattening over his flashing eyes. "I'm *selfish?*"

"Oh, I know I'm not innocent." She snorted derisively, shining the relentless spotlight on herself and thinking of all the times and ways she'd wronged his wife and the mother of his children, a woman she'd never even met and who had certainly never done anything to harm her. When karma swung back around in Gloria's direction, it was surely going to give her a big bite in the ass. "Trust me, I know. I'm ashamed. I have to live with that. I deserve the guilt."

"Look," he said, rubbing a hand over the top of his head and clearly thinking hard. "Look…we both need some time to think—"

"Oh, I don't need any time," she assured him. "The

only thing I'm thinking is thank God your wife never knew about us. It would've hurt her for no good reason." She paused. "Well, that and thank God we always used condoms." Crossing to the door, she opened it for him. "Goodbye, Aaron."

For a few seconds he seemed too stunned to move, but then he got his body in gear and walked toward her, his steps slow and deliberate. Then he was in her face again, dimpling with the self-assurance that had undoubtedly helped him float through life with minimal thought to how his actions affected others.

"You'll be back." The confident gleam that she knew so well crept back into his eyes as he stepped over the threshold and turned to face her. "There ain't a man out there that can make you come like I can. You'll be back."

A startled burst of laughter hit her, hard, before she managed to choke it back. What a narcissistic SOB she'd hooked herself up with. Why had she never seen it before? The sad thing was, he really believed that nonsense. Luckily, she was just the woman to burst his oversize bubble.

"Oh, honey," she said, reining in her smile and dropping her voice. With exquisite care, she straightened his tie and smoothed the lapels of his lab coat. "I thought you knew. I can buy a vibrator that'll be twice as effective as you and only half the hassle. Bye, now."

In the most deliciously satisfying moment of her life, she shut the door in his shocked face. Then she turned back around, swiped her hands together—good riddance—and surveyed her office.

She was no longer hungry, so she dumped the oatmeal in the trash. But she was still a little agitated, and her office didn't feel quite right after his unwelcome invasion. In fact, it felt contaminated. Not that there was much she could do about it, since she had to see her first patient in a few minutes. And it wasn't as if she had a priest on speed dial. Otherwise, she'd call him in to perform a quick exorcism of Aaron's spirit, both from her office and her life.

But she did have air freshener and hand sanitizer.

She liberally spritzed the air with her laundry-fresh spray, then squirted a full tablespoon of her industrial-strength sanitizer in her hands. She worked it in, which was the rough equivalent of dunking her hands in undiluted bleach, then took a deep breath, feeling slightly better already.

But, man, it was hot in here. She pressed both hands to her cheeks and discovered that she was crying. Not an ugly cry, though. Just a few random tears that were a lingering memento of what had already been a very emotional day.

And it wasn't even noon yet.

"Wow, Glo," she murmured to herself, shaking her head. "You're a real mess, you know that? A real freaking mess. And to think they gave you a medical license. First rule of pulling it together? Stop talking to yourself."

She shut up.

There. That was a step in the right direction.

But she couldn't very well greet her patients looking as if she'd been crying. So she swerved into her private bathroom and was using a tissue to mop up the blotchy mascara patches under her eyes when her phone vibrated in her lab coat pocket.

Normally, if someone called her right before an appointment, she'd let it go to voice mail. But the possibility that it might be Cooper was too enticing to pass up, and she had the phone in her hand by the middle of the second vibration.

Her pulse kicked into overdrive when she saw the display.

"Cooper," she said, trying not to sound flustered. "Hi."

"You sound funny," he told her.

Cooper, she was beginning to realize, was a man of few words, and *hello* and *goodbye* didn't seem to be on his list. He was also unusually perceptive, as though no fine detail of her behavior was beneath his notice, and that was disconcerting.

"I do not sound funny. And we don't know each other well enough for you to know whether I sound funny or not."

He made a disbelieving sound. Did a smirk have a sound? Because if so, it'd sound just like that.

"We'll get back to that. What'd the doctor say about Talia?"

"The usual," she said. "They're doing blood work and scans. We should know more by the end of the day."

"Waiting sucks."

"Yeah. But her oncologist's a good guy and he won't mess around. So she's in great hands. And guess what—Tony showed up at her appointment and asked her to marry him. He had the ring and everything! So now they're engaged! But don't mention it until Tony tells you."

"You're happy for her?"

"Very happy for her. She deserves some happiness."

"So do you, Doc. So why did you sound funny when you picked up?"

There he went again, sniffing out all her secrets like some sort of emotional bloodhound.

"It's not even worth getting into." She fidgeted with agitation, checking her watch and smoothing her skirt. "Forget it. So do you have a breakfast meeting?"

There was a pause.

"I can wait," he said.

"Fine," she snapped. "If you must know, nosy, Aaron was just here."

Longer pause.

"Yeah?" he asked, his voice tight. "How'd that go?"

"I can't get into it. I have patients waiting."

There. She sounded very firm and official, and that should put an end to the third degree.

A low rumbling sound suspiciously like a growl came from his end of the line.

"You're like a dog with a bone, Eagle Scout. You know that?"

He ignored this insult with the single-minded focus of a bloodhound. With a bone.

"What did the guy want, Gloria?"

"He wants me back," she told him. "He always wants what he doesn't have at the moment."

"Is that so?" he said in a voice like splintered ice. "And where do you stand on that? Now that you've had a couple nights to sleep on it?"

"I told him to get out. I'm done with him."

"What?" Cooper asked. "You did?"

"Yeah. It's over."

Cooper hesitated. "You don't just wrap up a two-year relationship, even a bad one, in a single conversation."

"I'm. Done. With. Him."

A sharp exhalation followed by a shaky laugh. "I'm glad to hear it," Cooper said.

Chapter 7

Two nights later, Gloria lay in bed in a wired and exhausted stupor. Flat on her belly with her head and one arm dangling over the side, she watched the sharp blue display on her alarm clock.

One forty-seven.

She hadn't been sleeping well. To make things worse, today's surgeries had kicked her butt, leaving her wrung out and stressed. A liposuction patient had developed a bleeding complication, scaring them all for several tense moments. Another patient, a scheduled breast reduction, had to be canceled because her blood pressure wasn't stable.

This wasn't how she'd imagined spending her life all those years ago, in the backbreaking days when she'd worked and clawed her way through college, medical school and her residency. She'd never thought she'd be spending all her time and training helping rich women in their relentless quest for ageless physical perfection. She'd thought she'd help people who'd been burned or otherwise disfigured in accidents. She'd thought she'd mend the precious faces of children born with cleft palates. She'd thought she'd spend her days doing something worthwhile that made her proud of herself.

That was her problem these days. She didn't know what it felt like to be proud of herself.

Then there was Talia. Always Talia.

She stared at the clock.

Still one forty-seven.

Tonight's bath hadn't helped her unwind, nor had the mug of hot milk and honey, nor had the second mug of hot milk and honey, this one liberally laced with brandy.

Nothing helped.

Her eyes were gritty, her shoulders knotted and her nerves frayed.

Cooper hadn't called again.

One forty-seven.

Over on the nightstand, her phone buzzed, its bright display dissipating the shadows and lighting up the bedroom. Startled, she snapped to attention, scrambled up to sitting and grabbed the phone.

Cooper, she saw, feeling a swoop of relief so powerful it scared her. She hadn't realized how much she liked hearing from him or that she'd been waiting for it.

"Hey," she said.

"Sorry to call so late. Are you sleeping?"

"No."

"I was hoping…"

"Yeah?"

"You didn't think about me today, did you?"

Gloria couldn't admit the truth, but she couldn't manage a breezy lie either. Her hesitation probably told him everything he needed to know.

"So I forgot to mention," he said, his voice a low rumble in her ear, so close that it was almost as though he was here in the room—in the bed—with her, "I'll be home on Friday."

Her heart began doing a funny staccato thing.

"Yeah?"

"Yeah. So you could have dinner with me."

She shouldn't be this tempted, and for one fleeting second she hated him for seeing inside her, exploiting her weaknesses and showing her again—as if she could ever forget—what a mess she was. Having an affair with a married man and then, just when she grew enough brains to get out of that bad situation, thinking about another man. Wishing he would call. Wanting to see him again. When had she become one of those despised women who couldn't survive for two seconds without a man by her side?

What was she doing?

How was she ever going to be proud of herself if she never stood on her own two feet?

"I can't," she told him.

"You can't eat?"

"I can't have dinner with you."

"You're right," he agreed. "Dinner's way too significant, and I don't want you thinking I like you too much."

God, she thought, grinning even though she didn't want to. Why was he so disarming?

"Cooper—"

"Lunch, then. Lunch has no significance as a social convention. It's just lunch."

"I'm a disaster right now, Cooper. You know this. You shouldn't even want to spend time with me."

"I'm a disaster, too. I'm a workaholic. I have issues about being adopted. And I haven't cleaned out my sock drawer in months. Years, probably. So have lunch with me."

Catching herself just before she began to laugh, she gave herself a swift mental kick in the ass. Focus. She needed to focus. "I can't."

"Gloria—"

"I can't. Please understand."

A harsh sigh. "So you don't think about me?"

Did she think about him? Please. Was Times Square overrun with tourists?

"That's not the issue."

"It's the only issue, Doc."

The rising frustration in his voice hardened her resolve. She couldn't play with his emotions or send mixed signals or jerk Cooper around the way Aaron had jerked her around. She wasn't going to do it.

"I need to figure out why I'm so screwed up." There it was, right on the table for all to see: her biggest shame. "I need to figure out who I am and what I need. And I can't do it if I go straight from him to you."

For the longest five seconds of her life, he didn't say anything.

"If you don't want me hanging around," he told her, his voice husky, "then tell me not to call you anymore. It's easy."

She took a deep breath and, for once in her life, did the smart thing.

"Don't call me anymore."

Thumbing the off button, she dropped the phone to the carpeted floor with a soft thunk, resumed her belly-down, arm-dangling position on the bed and stared at the clock with gritty eyes.

One fifty-one.

Two Months Later
Jackson Hole, Wyoming

Cooper topped off his bourbon, sipped half of it and did another lap around his huge room, growing more agitated with each step. He and his brother, Marcus, had flown out west to Sweet Heaven, the over-the-top ranch owned by one of their clients, Judah Cross. Judah, an aging rocker with enough hard-living mileage to give Mick Jagger and Steven Tyler a run for their money, had invited them, along with Claudia Montgomery, who worked at a competing auction house, to his home to be vetted. Judah wanted them to "peel back the layers" so he could "get to know their souls" and thereby decide which auction house was worthy of handling his memorabilia sale.

Which basically meant that Judah was requiring everyone to jump through a lot of hoops and listen to his woo-woo existential B.S. before he awarded anyone his business.

Since the memorabilia was worth at least 20 million, they'd all sucked it up and attended Judah's bonfire tonight—yes, bonfire, with hot dogs, s'mores and even bison burgers—and talked about their innermost secrets.

Fun had not been had by all. The process had been the rough equivalent of being caught peeing in a public elevator, and he was not keen to repeat it.

Ever.

Finishing the last of his bourbon, he savored the trail of heat down his throat and swiped the back of his hand over his mouth.

Oh, yeah, he thought as his head went a little fuzzier, taking the edge off his taut nerves. Judah stocked the good stuff. One of the benefits of being a rock god, Cooper supposed.

From down the hall came the distant sounds of a woman's breathy cries of passion and a man's low rumbling answer, noises that made Cooper want to smother himself with a pillow.

Instead he crossed back to the liquor tray and refilled his glass, but he could still hear them. He could still. Freaking. Hear. Them.

Not that he wasn't happy for Marcus and Claudia. The two of them had clearly hit it off and made a good pair, with sparks flying off their skin every time they looked at each other. He'd noticed it earlier and had a grand old time needling Marcus about her.

So the two of them, at least, were enjoying a pleasant end to bonfire night.

Whoopee for them. That didn't mean he wanted to hear them make each other come until the sun came up.

He, on the other hand, had not had a good night, nor had he had a good day, nor a good night's sleep in the two months since Gloria gave him the kiss-off. He had not enjoyed a meal, a glass of wine, a TV show or another woman's body since that terrible day. Oh, he'd backed off and given Gloria the space she requested, and for that he should be awarded another Eagle badge, if not a Nobel Prize. He was quite the gentleman, all right.

He was also a hollowed-out shell of his former self and a mere paper cut away from a complete breakdown.

Gloria.

Gloria…Gloria…*Gloria*.

He hadn't seen her. Which of course meant that she was all he could see.

How was she doing? Had she gotten back together with— *Shit*. He couldn't even allow himself to think the man's name; it hurt way too much.

Most important, did Gloria ever think of Cooper?

Could she possibly miss him?

Probably not. He knew that. They barely knew each other.

But still…

He thought about her.

No. It was worse than that.

She was under his skin…inside his brain…flowing through his blood.

Which was why he needed another drink.

And the reason his need for her was so acute tonight, he thought, refilling his glass and sloshing a little over the sides—damn, he hated to waste good bourbon like that; with no napkin in sight, he wiped it up with the edge of his sleeve—was that Judah had forced him to think about her at the bonfire. Judah had needled and badgered him until he'd admitted it aloud, in front of everyone: he considered Gloria his woman.

She wasn't ready for it, which was probably why she was essentially running in the opposite direction.

But she was his. Would officially be his one day soon if he had anything to say about it. The certainty was there inside him, buried deep, like the cells in his marrow.

His.

So what did this fixation on a woman he hadn't seen in sixty-three days say about him? That he was out of touch with reality? A stalker? Insane?

All of those, probably.

After he'd admitted his feelings for her at the bonfire, Judah had reminded him that life was short and encouraged him to—what was the phrase?—climb down off the mountain and get his woman. He'd even given Cooper a good-luck charm to help him on his way: a jade dragon pendant that was now hanging

around Cooper's neck. Cooper rubbed the dragon between his thumb and forefinger. The thing did make
him feel a little better, to tell the truth, and he'd take
any and all infusions of courage he could get.

God, he missed her.

He'd be back in New York in the next couple of
days, at which point he'd figure out his grand strategy for getting Gloria to give him a chance. That was
if he could survive another couple of days with this
oppressive loneliness dragging him down. At some
point he'd started to feel as though he was living his
life in a swimming pool, battling the water's resis-
tance and his lungs' lack of air to accomplish even
the smallest tasks.

A few days seemed like a long time from now.

Too long.

Flopping back onto the bed spread-eagled, he
stared at the rough-hewn beams across the ceiling
and tried to decide what he should do.

He could wait until he got back to New York in a
few days, or he could send her flowers, or he could…
he could…

Call her. Right now.

Brilliant idea. Quite possibly the best he'd ever had.

Bolting back up again, he grabbed his cell phone
from the nightstand, punched the number and listened,
his heart cartwheeling through his chest.

Ringing. Her phone was ringing…ringing…

"Hello," she said.

"Hey, Doc, hi. It's me," he began, grinning idioti-
cally. "Cooper—"

"You've reached Gloria Adams—"

Voice mail. His heart fell through his chest wall, crashing and burning into a pile of ash.

"I'm not available right now, so please leave a message. Thanks!"

Beep.

He hesitated. What now? Leave a message? No message?

Message, for sure. No guts, no glory, right?

"Gloria, hi. It's Cooper. And it's, ah—" He checked his watch. "It's one in the morning. I'm in, ah, Jackson Hole. Wyoming. Business trip. I guess that makes it pretty late in the city. What's the time difference? Three hours? Sorry about that. You're probably sleeping. Unless you're screening my call." He paused. "I choose to believe that you're there and you're alone, because I don't want my head to, you know, explode. So are you there?"

He waited, hoping she'd have mercy and spare him from the indignity of leaving what was turning out to be a rambling message, but there was only silence.

Right.

Well, get to the point, lover boy.

"So, the thing is," he continued, sitting on the edge of the bed, "I can't stop thinking about you. I. Cannot. Stop. Thinking. About. You. And I know I'm not, I don't know, Prince Harry or someone fantastic like that, but I'm not a bad-looking guy, and I've got all my teeth and a good job and a great family, and I'm a...a... What's the term? Oh, yeah, I'm a monogamist, and I'd never cheat on you, in case you're worried about that."

Sighing, he fell back and resumed his spread-eagle position on the bed.

"It'd be pretty hard for me to cheat on you," he said on a shaky laugh. "I don't think I've noticed another woman since I laid eyes on you. Your face is all I can see."

Silence.

Sudden exhaustion washed over him, exacerbating his yearning for her. He let his eyes roll closed and his thoughts drift. His voice turned hoarse.

"I remember everything about you, Gloria. I remember your big brown eyes and the way you smile and the way you have that one dimple that's a little bit deeper than the one on the other side. You smell like flowers and coconuts. I remember that real well. You have this tough, take-no-prisoners shell, and you're smart, and you're so determined to keep me away, and I get that. I really do. You're coming off of a toxic relationship, and you're thinking maybe I'm toxic, too, and I guess you're smart to be suspicious."

He broke off, swallowing hard because his mouth had gone dry and he wasn't at all sure he was saying this right.

"But the thing is, Gloria, I can't control when I met you. If I could've met you two years ago or five years ago, don't you think I would've taken that option? I can't help what happened to you before. I can only tell you how I feel, you know? I can only tell you what

I'll do and what I won't do. And then I can show you so you'll know for sure."

His throat felt raw now. Hot. Tight.

And he was so tired. As though he had nothing left, because he was pouring everything—all his energy, everything he was—into the phone and this one chance to get the woman he needed.

"And here's what I know for sure, Doc. I will treasure you. *Treasure.* You know how I know that? Because I can't breathe without—"

Beeeeeep.

Well, wasn't that just great, he thought, rolling over onto his side and covering his eyes with his arm, the phone still clutched in his hand. The machine had cut him off.

Typical.

He drifted off to sleep and startled himself awake a few hours later.

His head felt as if it'd been fed through a meat grinder.

"Ah, shit," he said, sitting up and squinting against the bright sunlight flooding the room. His eyes didn't want to be open, but closed was no better because they felt as though they'd been filled with broken glass, and every tiny movement seemed to scrape his corneas. He raised a hand to his forehead to see if that would stop the pounding, and that was when he noticed that he was holding something small and hard.

Lowering his hand, he stared blankly at his cell phone as disjointed details from last night swirled back to him. The bonfire…the bourbon…the overwhelming desire to speak to Gloria…

He stilled, frozen behind a wall of rising horror, the phone gripped in his hand.

He hadn't…he hadn't *drunk-dialed* Gloria, had he?

Yeah.

He was pretty sure he had.

"Fuuuuuuuck," he said, chucking the phone across the room.

Chapter 8

"Morning, Liz." Cooper strode through the reception area outside his office at Davies & Sons in Manhattan two days later, waving to his receptionist as he went. "Miss me?"

"Cried into my pillow every night." Liz yawned and didn't bother looking away from her computer screen as her fingers danced over the keyboard. "Did you bring me something from the Wild West? I need a souvenir for holding down the fort in your absence."

"Of course," he said, tossing her a bag of huckleberry hard candies for the jar she kept on her desk. "Huckleberries are big in Wyoming for some reason."

"Thank youuuu," she sang, nabbing them with a neat one-handed catch before resuming typing.

"What'd I miss?" He paused to peruse the stack of

mail she'd left for him to see, switching his briefcase to his free hand. He checked his watch and decided he had time for a couple of quick calls before he went into the weekly meeting with Marcus and their cousins Tony and Sandro, the other owners of Davies & Sons. "Any fires to put out before my nine-thirty?"

"No fires." Liz stopped typing and looked up at him, an amused gleam in her eye. "But you do have a visitor."

Cooper had taken a couple more steps toward his office, but now he frowned over his shoulder at her. "Did I forget something?"

"Nope." Liz was looking at him and grinning now, and that made him nervous. "She said she didn't have an appointment but that she hoped you could squeeze her in."

"Well, who is it?" he asked impatiently, checking his watch again. "I don't really have time for twenty questions."

"A Gloria Adams." Liz's honey sweetness was laced with mischief, as though she suspected she was dropping a bomb into the middle of his life. "Do you know her?"

"Wait, what?" he asked faintly, his brain emptying of all rational thought.

"Glo-ri-*a* Ad-*ams*." Liz was downright gleeful now as she slid her chair back and stood. "I'll get rid of her, though. I know how busy you are."

"Like hell you will," he muttered, thrusting his briefcase at her as he headed for his office. "And can you buzz Marc and tell him I'll be late? Thanks."

Liz's low chuckle was the last thing he heard as he slipped into his office.

Gloria, who'd been over at the windows behind his desk admiring the view, spun to face him. Their gazes connected, and he felt instantly lighter, almost euphoric. The morning sun hit her eyes just right, making them sparkle with light, an effect that was magnified when one corner of her mouth turned up as she dimpled at him. Another tiny part of him fell helplessly—irrevocably—under her control. It was just gone; he wasn't getting it back. And it occurred to him that if she'd come by to announce, say, that she was getting a restraining order to keep him from ever contacting her again, he probably wouldn't survive.

"Hi," he managed, clicking the door shut behind him.

"Hi."

He waited, giving her a beat or two to explain why she was there. During their past encounters, he'd had a tendency to come on too strong, and he needed to keep a lid on that. The last thing he wanted to do was scare her away again before she even gave him a chance.

"You look amazing," he blurted. It was true, even if he hadn't meant to toss it out there like that. There was something subtly different about her, as though she held her head a little higher or glowed with more vitality or something. She wore a blue dress that hit her in all the right places, and heels, which meant she was probably on her way to the hospital. And she'd done something to her hair, because it framed her face and she had bangs now, making her more arresting than ever. And here he was, watching her the way a leopard watches a baby gazelle frolic through the grass, all but slobbering. Did he have moves or what? "I mean…it's great to see you."

She stared at him, her expression unreadable.

Shit, he thought. Shit, shit, *shit.* There he went again, coming on too strong. Why not just throw her over his shoulder, haul her back to his cave and be done with it? Why couldn't he play it cool where this one woman was concerned? Why did he have to act like the world's biggest idiot?

"That's funny," she said. "I was just thinking that you look amazing. And it's great to see you."

He blinked, trying to get his head around that. When he couldn't, he decided it was best to just ask her outright.

"Is this a trick?"

"I tell you it's great to see you, and you ask if it's a trick?"

"I'm surprised to see you. Especially after I, ah…"

"Drunk-dialed me the other night?"

"I did, in fact, drunk-dial you the other night, yes."

She moved toward him, her gaze searching. "You said a lot of things. Do you remember?"

As if he could forget the way he'd stripped his soul bare and put it on a silver platter for her to see.

"Yep," he said, running a hand over his nape.

Something in her expression seemed to dim, as though she'd never really expected him to have strong feelings about her anyway, and this confirmed it.

"So you regret it, then," she said quietly. "You didn't mean it."

Well, there it was: the perfect opportunity to disown what he'd said. If he wanted to.

Only he didn't want to.

He moved toward her. "I don't regret anything. I meant it. I mean it."

Though she didn't quite smile, the light came back on in her face. "So I thought I'd update you on my life a little bit."

The segue caught him off guard. Did this mean they were…? What did this mean?

"Update?"

"Yes. I've been working. Well, I'm always working, so that's not new, but I've been cutting back on the rhinoplasties and breast augmentations and face-lifts and working with a foundation that helps children born with cleft palates. I love it. It's amazing. It's what I've been wanting to do for a long time."

"That's fantastic, Gloria."

She beamed at him. "I knew you'd be happy for me. And I've been spending a lot of time with Talia while she goes through her treatments. She's doing great."

"I know. Tony keeps us posted. She's all he talks about."

"They want to get married in Bora-Bora in a few months. I've been helping with the planning."

"I know." That was all well and good, but what did it have to do with him and Gloria? Still, he played along. "I've got my white linen on standby."

She paused. He waited, on high alert for the only thing that mattered.

"I haven't seen Aaron."

His heart made like a balloon, swelling in his chest until there was no room for breath.

"Well, I've run into him a few times at the hospital. And he's tried to—"

"He wants you back," he said dully, knowing nothing in life—not his life, anyway—could ever be that easy. And as someone who had pretty much lost his mind over this woman, he knew how the other guy must feel. "He's desperate to get you back."

She shrugged that away. "That's his problem. I'm not mad at him. I'm not anything about him, except that now I see him for what he is." She took another step closer. "He had his chance already, and he blew it, so I don't care what he wants. Only what I want matters."

That balloon inside him expanded again, making him light-headed.

"And what's that?" he asked.

A pretty flush crept over her face. "I want to spend a little time with you. Get to know you better." He cocked his head, wanting to make sure he'd heard right. "I think you've got potential, Eagle Scout. I want to find out for sure."

This wasn't a declaration of undying love, but it was still one of the best things he'd ever heard.

"Come here," he said, weak with relief as he reached for her.

They came together in front of his desk. The second he touched her, all his ideas about not overwhelming her went right out his floor-to-ceiling windows. Holding her face between his hands, he burrowed his fingers into the heavy satin of her hair, feeling for the warmth of her scalp underneath. There was only time for two words before he angled her head back and kissed her.

"Thank you."

Their mouths fit together, tentative at first, a slow, testing slide of lips so they could get the feel of each other and get past the electric sensation of being in each other's arms.

And then his mind blanked out and his body took over.

Part of it was that she was so fragrant—flowers and coconuts; he'd missed that heady combination—and so soft and yielding and, somehow, an aggressive wildcat. Plus, she made these breathy little mewling sounds that shot straight to the center of his brain, intoxicating him.

He lost his head a little.

He was always losing his head with her.

Groaning, he pulled her closer, running his hands down her supple back and hips, grabbing that ass to anchor her while he ground his swelling erection against the sweet spot between her legs. She was right there with him, hooking a knee around his thigh to keep him there, and, honest to God, he felt something pop inside his brain.

His hands went to work with no coherent instruction from him, stroking up her bare thighs and under her skirt, hefting her up so she could wrap her legs around his waist as he swung her around and plopped her on his desk.

Something hit the floor with a crash; he didn't bother looking to see what it was.

All that mattered was her open mouth as it worked beneath his, and her sharp little nails raking his nape and scalp, pulling his hair, and the way she parted her thighs for him, welcoming him, and he swore to himself—*swore it*—that he would be the last man to ever occupy this space with her.

This space was made for him.

She was made for him, and a part of him had known that the second he laid eyes on her.

"Wait." She pulled back, lids heavy and eyes glazed with passion. He followed her, recapturing that lush mouth because he'd waited so long to taste it. But she seemed to be coming to her senses. "Wait, Cooper. Aren't we at your office?"

"I'm with *you*." Since she wouldn't let him kiss her mouth, he took the opportunity to explore a little, planting his hands on either side of her torso so that his thumbs were in easy reach of her nipples, which he rubbed. She shuddered. Gasped. "I'm with *you*," he said again. "That's all I know."

"Cooper." Resting her palms on the desk for support, she let her head fall back, exposing the smooth column of her throat. Knowing an opportunity when he saw one, he leaned forward, licking it. "Cooper. Stop. Sto-op. This isn't taking it slow. *Cooper!*"

"Screw *slow*."

She put her hands on his chest and shoved him, hard.

"Yeah, okay." Sighing harshly, he let her go. "Okay, okay."

Feeling wrung out, if not ruined, and deciding it would be best if he put a little physical distance between them, he walked around to the other side of his desk, slumped into his chair, leaned back so he could rest his feet on the desk and closed his eyes, trying to get his overheated body under control. The continued sound of her breath, as though she was as far gone as he was, didn't exactly help. The situation called for drastic action, so he pinched the bridge of his nose until stars popped behind his lids.

There. That was better.

Opening his eyes, he saw Gloria still perched on the edge of his desk, her face lowered and shadowed.

"What?" he asked gently.

"I just feel like we should talk about the race thing. Before we go too far down this road."

"The race thing?" he echoed blankly. "What's that?"

She frowned, swiveling to face him. "Have we met? I'm black and you're white, Cooper."

His frazzled brain was having a tough time keeping up. "I'm well aware of my color, thanks. I'm the only white face in a black family, remember? What's your point?"

Her frown turned to a gape, as though she never could've imagined the existence of someone this clueless.

"My point is, I'm wondering if, I don't know, you only date sisters or something."

Yeah, okay. He got it. And she was starting to piss him off.

"Maybe you've got some fetish," she continued. "Maybe I'm your walk on the wild side before you settle down and marry Buffy Whitington from Greenwich."

"Or maybe you're not," he said, not bothering to keep the edge out of his voice.

She plowed ahead anyway. "But have you dated other black women? Do I remind you of the big love of your life—the one that got away? Am I your type?"

"No. No. Yes. Well, no. Anything else I can clarify for you?"

"I'm not your type?" Hurt flashed across her face before she quickly blanked out her expression. "So what's your type, then?"

"Normally? Petite blondes, if you must know."

"Petite blondes."

His lips thinned. He probably needed to work on his patience, because this seemed to be an important topic to her. But his body was a hive of buzzing hormones right now and, besides that, wasn't this the twenty-first freaking century? Why were they going there?

"Anything else I can help you with?" he snapped. "Do you want to know my number, too? Because if you do, I've got a lot of adding to do—"

"No! I do not want to know how many women you've been with!"

"What's with the twenty questions?" he wondered. "It's not like I'm your type, am I?"

Her face reddened like the burners on a stove. "I'm asking the questions here."

"Let me guess." He tried to smile, but his face felt as though it was encased in concrete. "Tall, dark and handsome, right?" She glanced quickly away, making a production out of smoothing her hair behind her ears and trying not to look guilty as charged. "Well, I'm tall and handsome. I'm not dark. Just so we're clear."

"Got it. Thanks," she said sourly.

They glared across the desk at each other, trapped in a moody silence while he wondered how things had taken such a sharp left turn into ugly territory.

"So...this thing." She gestured between them. "With us—"

"It's called a relationship, Gloria. Our developing relationship. You should practice saying it. Get used to the whole idea. I'd hoped you were used to it, since it's been a long damn time coming."

"Our relationship has a short shelf life, then." There was a distinct bite in her voice now. "We're not each other's types, so we'll never last, right? I guess that's fine with me."

A muscle started to work in the back of his jaw. *"Fine?"*

"I just want to know going in— Stop glaring at me like that!"

"Here's what you need to know." He dropped his feet from the desk, scooted his chair closer and leaned in, staring up at her. *"You're* my type. If you came in green, I'd want you in green. My heart and my dick don't care what color you are or that our colors don't match. Got it?"

She faltered. "Yeah, but—"

"But what? I'm just a dumb white boy who's incapable of figuring out who he wants or what color she is?"

"What? No! It's just that…I've never dated a white guy before."

"Well, neither have I," he said flatly.

That broke up some of the tension. She snorted but didn't laugh.

"What's this about, Gloria?"

She hesitated. "Relationships are hard enough when everyone comes from the same demographic group."

"Do me a favor, Doc."

"What?"

"Shut up and stop thinking."

"Excuse me? Do you want me to go ethnic on your ass?"

That made him grin, because now she sounded like Mama. Which made him think that it'd be a good idea to get the two women in his life together. "You can think about your patients and Talia and her wedding and all, but don't think about this." He gestured between them. "Just let it happen. It's happening. Okay?"

"I have to get to work. I'm late." A hint of a smile softened the edges of her mouth. "And since I'm smarter after Aaron, I'm not sleeping with you until we get to know each other much better. Just so you know."

He suppressed a grin with difficulty. Taking one of her hands, he raised it to his lips so he could suck and then bite the tender webbing between her thumb and index finger. She gasped, shivering.

"We'll see about that," he murmured.

Chapter 9

Gloria hurried into the café a couple blocks from the hospital and saw at a glance that Cooper was already there.

Typical, she thought, grinning as she hurried through the double glass doors and headed for his table, which was near the soaring windows. The lingering Eagle Scout in him did not, apparently, allow him to ever be late. In the two months since they'd been dating, he'd never been so much as thirty seconds tardy and usually beat her to wherever they were going.

She liked that about him.

She liked pretty much everything about him, and that was what worried her.

He'd already ordered his standard drink, iced tea

with lemon, and had the menu open on the table in front of him. His blond head was bent low over his phone as he checked his email, and she had a minute to study him as she wove her way through the crowded tables.

Today he wore a black T-shirt with jeans so faded and weathered they'd be white with another wash or two. His long body was relaxed, slung back in the chair with his ankles crossed, and his shoulders seemed to span the width of the table. His arms, meanwhile, were works of art, muscled and cut so powerfully that she really should put some effort into figuring out how to capture his physicality and offer it to her patients. If she could develop a surgical procedure to make other men look the way he did, she'd make a fortune by the end of the year, no question.

His lids were lowered so that his lashes, which were dark and lush, fanned the sharp planes of his cheeks. And then, as though he felt her presence when she came within a few feet of the table, his bright gaze flicked up and connected with hers.

A transformation came over him.

He smiled, a wide ear-to-ear grin of pleasure, and all his harsh masculinity receded in favor of boyish delight. Dimples grooved in his cheeks, and lines appeared at the corners of his shining blue eyes. Watching him, she felt that thing she felt whenever they saw each other—that delicious swoop of pleasure that exactly mirrored what she was seeing on his face.

It was as though life went on all the time, but *living* happened only when they were together.

In one smooth motion, he put his phone down, slid his chair out and stood, reaching out a hand to bring her close, as though there could possibly be some other place she might slip off to when he was in the room.

When he bent his head to kiss her, it was, like all his greeting kisses, lingering, sweet and unabashed. She'd thought more than once that even if he ever had a private meeting with the president and she interrupted it, he'd be this glad to see her and would welcome her just like this.

And when the kiss was over, he folded her into his arms for a bear hug, lifting her to the tips of her toes, then, finally, he let her go with a kiss in that tender space right where her cheek met her ear and whispered the same thing he always told her and that she never got tired of hearing: "I missed you."

She did the same thing she always did: ducked her head, smoothed her hair and flushed furiously. Because she could never get past the idea that this was all temporary. That she'd better not get too attached, because he'd get wise to her soon or find someone else soon, and then he'd be gone and she'd be crushed. That it was better to never show too much emotion where men were concerned, and it was much, much better to never hint to Cooper Davies that she might be falling in love with him.

She tried not to let her smile show that she counted the minutes in between their time together, waiting until she could see him and breathe again.

"Don't get mushy on me, Eagle Scout."

Usually when she said this, the light in his big baby blues dimmed just a bit, but he recovered quickly and joked away the hurt, saying something like, "I'm all about the mush, Doc." But this time he caught her hand, stopping her when she would've slid into her chair.

Trapped and wary, she met his unsmiling eyes and waited.

"And you missed me, too," he prompted, bending his knees just enough to put them at eye level.

She opened her mouth. Her brain knew that saying words that were true and meant so much to him wouldn't kill her, but her gut—her still-healing heart—wasn't so sure.

"You missed me, too," he repeated softly.

Her smile widened just a little, and there was no stopping it. "I...missed you, too."

Those eyes crinkled at her. "Was that so hard?"

"You have no idea."

Leaning in, he kissed her again, tenderly, then pulled out her chair so she could sit.

That was when she noticed the steaming bowl of clam chowder and let out a tiny squeal of glee that could barely be heard over her growling stomach. "Is this for me?"

"It is."

"God bless you, you wonderful man! How did you know?"

"I'm psychic. Or maybe it's that you order clam chowder whenever it's on a menu and then spend the rest of the meal waxing poetic about it."

"I do like to wax." She grabbed her cloth napkin and put it in her lap. "How was your morning? What've you been up to?"

"Nothing much," he said, shrugging as he took a sip of tea. "Meeting. Conference call. Another meeting. The usual. How'd surgery go?"

"Perfect." She opened her menu and took a look. "I did a child with a cleft palate first thing. Then I had office appointments. I was able to talk a woman down from the watermelon-sized implants to three-quarter watermelon-sized. So it was a huge victory. Now her back will only ache most of the time instead of all the time. But, hey, her thirty-years-older husband is happy, so that's all that really matters, right?"

"I want you to know," he said solemnly, picking up his own menu, "that I am very happy with the size of your breasts."

"I'm so glad," she said, laughing.

"I'm deeply unhappy about how little I get to see your breasts, but their size is perfect— Oh, the salmon looks good."

This was a theme that had turned into a running joke. No one was more surprised than Gloria that they'd held out this long on having sex when their chemistry was this explosive, but she'd been serious about getting to know him better first, and he seemed serious about taking things as slowly as she needed.

"Is that so?" Keeping her gaze lowered, she flipped a page. "Well, we'll have to do something about that, won't we? Oh, they have risotto. Did you see that?"

"Yeah, I was thinking about the risotto— Wait, what? What did you say?"

"Hmm?" she said absently, trying to keep a straight face. "I was saying I might get the risotto—"

"No," he said urgently, laying his menu down. "We were definitely talking about your breasts. I remember stuff like that."

"Hello," interrupted their server, smiling at Gloria. "Welcome! Can I get you started on a drink or an appetizer?"

"I'll have a diet cola, please." Gloria pointed to the third and fourth settings at the table. "And you can go ahead and take those if you want to. We won't be needing—"

"Actually, we will," Cooper interrupted.

"I'll be right back, then," the server said, and left.

Gloria raised her brows at him. "You didn't say anyone else was joining us."

"No?" Cooper said, studiously avoiding her gaze.

Now she was beginning to get suspicious. "Who is it?"

He waved a hand, keeping his eyes on the menu. "Just my parents," he said breezily.

That bombshell soared through the air and hit the ground beneath her feet with a reverberating clang. She cocked her head, wanting to make sure she heard the punch line when it came. But there didn't seem to be one.

"Your...*parents?*"

"Yeah. They're visiting for a couple days on their way to Capri."

Cooper's parents were retired and had made a cottage industry of traveling the world in search of the sunniest spot. In the time they'd been dating, they'd vacationed in Hawaii, Costa Rica and Greece, but they'd come nowhere near Manhattan. Their home base was in Palm Beach, so she'd had no chance to meet them, nor had Cooper ever suggested it.

In short, she'd had absolutely no freaking warning that she was about to meet Cooper's parents, and she had no idea how to react.

"You want me to meet *your parents?*"

"Of course I want you to meet my parents. Why does that surprise you?"

Because Aaron never had, nor had the smattering of other men she'd dated or hooked up with since her divorce.

"I haven't met that many parents in my dating life, to be honest."

"Well, that's about to change." His gaze flicked up, connecting with hers across the top of his menu. "Don't worry, though. You'll love them."

"Why didn't you give me some warning?"

"This is the warning," he said. "I didn't want to give you time to obsess about it, which you're clearly doing."

The way he raked her with that intent gaze of his, sized her up and hit the nail on the head every time was profoundly unsettling. The only other person who'd ever been able to read her like that was Talia, and Talia was allowed because they were blood relations.

"You don't know me," she snapped.

Crooked smile. "Oh, I know you, Doc."

"A woman needs time to get her thoughts together before she meets—"

"Cut the bullshit, Glo. Before you give yourself a panic attack. You need to realize I'm serious about you." He paused, covering her fist where it lay on the table. "And if I'm serious about you, then my parents need to meet you. That's how the world works."

She fidgeted, wondering how her makeup was holding up and why she hadn't worn the blue dress rather than this flashier red one. Not that her appearance was the real issue.

"But what if they don't like me? Then is it just adios, Gloria? Have a nice life?"

He gaped. "Why wouldn't they like you?"

She tossed her hair and smiled with fake confidence, dredging up some bravado from somewhere. "You're right. They'll quickly see that I'm the best thing that's ever happened to you."

That made him frown for some reason.

"What? It's a joke, Cooper!"

"I know."

"So why the look?"

"Forget it." He studied her for a minute, and then his expression cleared. "If your parents were alive, I'd want to meet them. You know that, right?"

"If my parents were alive, the last thing I'd do is introduce you to them."

"Why?"

"My father was a lying cheat, and my mother was

a doormat," she said flatly. "And if you met them, you'd probably think less of me. Any other questions?"

"Yeah. Why are you always so sure I'm going to think less of you?"

Because most people eventually did think less of her, not that she was going to tell him that.

Once again, though, he seemed to know.

That was the thing about Cooper. He always just knew.

"You know what I see when I look at you?" he quietly asked her.

"The woman who can beat you in any field of athletic competition?" They'd been training to qualify for the next Boston together.

He grinned. "A fine athlete. Your marathon training times are quite good. I'll give you that."

She nodded regally. "I'll take that."

"I see an incredible woman. A strong, interesting, smart, beautiful and sexy woman."

"Why, thank you. And please stop there before you get to the *but*."

"Not a chance." He paused, then locked eyes with her. "And I see a woman who's so scared and vulnerable that she's determined to drive me away because she thinks I'll decide I don't want her."

That hit her like a roundhouse kick to the solar plexus.

She looked away, her smile fading as she focused on the dessert case so she wouldn't have to meet his gaze. There was no comeback for that, so she didn't try to manufacture one.

"Here's the thing you need to think about, Glo," he continued. "What if there's nothing I can find out about you that'll drive me away? What then?"

She turned back to him, their gazes connecting. Inside her, meanwhile, a tiny bloom of hope was beginning to blossom, and she didn't know if she wanted to water it or stomp it to smithereens before the inevitable droughts and locust plagues hit.

"What is it about you, Cooper?" she asked. Something in his intent expression softened, warming his sapphire eyes until she felt as if she could drown in them without regret. "Why do I always feel like I can believe you?"

"Because you can."

Her inner voice told her to leave it at that and keep her big mouth shut before she gave him the keys to the kingdom. Her heart told her to risk it.

Though her heart had a dismal track record, she decided to trust it, just this once.

"You know I'm already halfway in love with you, don't you?"

He planted his elbows on the table and leaned in, getting as close to her as he possibly could. "What can we do about that other 50 percent?"

She caught herself starting to smile and shook her head instead. "You won't be happy until you get it, will you?"

"No," he said, unsmiling. "With you? I want it all."

"So," she said, mirroring his posture and leaning closer. "We have this Judah Cross auction we're attending at the end of the week."

Interest flickered in his eyes. "Yeah?"

"I've been thinking."

"Do tell."

"Maybe you could come over for a drink or something after."

His gaze dropped to her mouth. *"Or something?"*

"Yeah," she said, standing halfway and tipping up her chin so he could kiss her. "A lot of *or something.*"

"You got it," he said with a smile as he kissed her.

"A-hem," said a woman's voice at the side of the table. "This can't be our son, can it, honey? Our son doesn't believe in PDAs."

"Looks like our son," rumbled a man's voice.

Oh, God.

Flaming with embarrassment, Gloria eased back and covered her mouth with her hand, as if that could erase Mrs. Davies's first impression of her as the woman who couldn't keep her lips to herself.

"Sorry," she said quickly, sliding her chair back and standing. "Hi. I'm Gloria. Adams. Gloria Adams. It's really nice to meet you both."

Whatever she'd expected, it wasn't these two. Mr. and Mrs. Davies—Ernest and Marlene—were both tall, lanky and youthful, as though they were Cooper's older siblings rather than his parents. Mr. Davies wore a bright blue T-shirt under a high-end hoodie with black jeans that were starched and pressed. His baseball cap, which he quickly whisked off his bald head, was from Jay Z's latest concert tour. He was a perfect older copy of Marcus, which meant he was brown-skinned, hard-jawed and goateed, with brown eyes that sparkled with mischief.

Mrs. Davies, who was eyeing Gloria with keen interest, was as tall as her husband, in the six-one-ish range, and had her auburn hair in a wispy pixie cut that curled around her forehead, nape and ears. Also brown-skinned, she wore a black pencil skirt with a leopard-print blouse that draped around a trim waist.

"You're *Dr.* Adams, aren't you?" she asked in a crisp voice, shaking Gloria's hand in her firm grip. "Plastic surgeon?"

"Plastic surgeon, yep. That's me. Call me Gloria, though."

Mrs. Davies released her hand and hugged Cooper, who'd stood and shaken his father's hand already. "She's beautiful," she told him in a stage whisper. "Looks athletic."

"She is athletic," Cooper told her. "She runs a 5K in thirty-one minutes."

"Thirty-one, eh?" Mr. Davies had now engulfed Gloria's hand in his own, which was the rough equivalent of putting her fingers in a vise grip and tightening it down several notches. He gave her a squinty-eyed look that told her exactly where Cooper had learned his competitive streak. "Is that on a flat course? Because I can do a flat course in twenty-eight, twenty-nine, no problem."

"That was San Francisco last year," Gloria told him.

He nodded, a new gleam of respect in his eyes. "You might need to keep this one, Cooper," he said over his shoulder as he finally turned Gloria's hand loose. She lowered her hand to her side and discreetly flexed her fingers, trying not to wince. "She sounds like a contender."

"Oh, she's a contender," Cooper said, giving Gloria a quick smile of encouragement. "She makes me work for every point I get."

Gloria, who was feeling a bit more relaxed, frowned at him. "You haven't gotten any points on me, Eagle Scout."

"See?" Cooper asked his parents as, laughing, they all took their seats.

"Have you run a full yet?" Mr. Davies scooted his chair closer to Gloria's as though he wanted to keep her full attention. "I qualified for Boston last year, but then I twisted my knee."

"I've run a couple," Gloria said. "I ran the Flying Pig in Cincinnati five years ago."

"Flying Pig." Another solemn nod from Mr. Davies. "That's hilly country there. What was your time?"

"Don't answer that, Gloria," Mrs. Davies said, rolling her eyes and leaning across her husband to cut him off. "If you encourage him, he'll start talking about his mini-Ironman training, and no one wants that. Trust me."

"I'm trying to get to know Cooper's girlfriend, woman," Mr. Davies said, looking affronted. "And I don't appreciate being cut off."

Gloria, meanwhile, caught Cooper's amused eyes across the table and raised her brow.

Yeah, he mouthed. *You're my girlfriend.*

She grinned, ducking her head and flushing.

"Oh, I don't care what you appreciate," Mrs. Davies said, flapping a hand at her husband. "That's enough about you. I have a question for you, Gloria."

Gloria snapped to attention. "What is it?"

Mrs. Davies tipped her head up and smoothed her chin with her French-manicured hands. "Do I need my throat done? My skin's gone all to hell. I look like a turkey on his way to Thanksgiving dinner. Look at this wattle."

"You do not have a wattle," Gloria told her, laughing. "You can trust me on that. I know wattles."

"Really?" Mrs. Davies beamed happily at her. "What about my eyes? Is there anything I can do about these bags underneath? How much would an eye lift set me back?"

Mr. Davies interjected before Gloria could answer. "You're not getting an eye lift, Marlene," he snapped. "Stop hogging Gloria. She doesn't want to talk shop with you. She's on her lunch break." He paused for a breath. "Gloria, you ever thought about an Ironman? How's your swimming?"

"Oh, for God's sake." Mrs. Davies heaved a long-suffering sigh. "We'll talk later, Gloria. Without the menfolk."

"Can't wait," Gloria said. "But right now I want to know what kind of little boy Cooper was. Tell me everything. I want to know about his grades, what kinds of buddies he ran with, sports, braces, girlfriends... anything you can remember."

"Unfortunately," Cooper interjected smoothly, flashing her a squinty-eyed look, "the folks will be unable to stay for lunch. Something has suddenly come up. Isn't that right, folks?"

"Don't even try it," Gloria told him. "Start with his old girlfriends, Mrs. Davies. In case he tries to cut us off again."

Mrs. Davies rested her elbows on the table, warming to the topic right away. "Well, there was this one girl in high school—"

"The stalker?" Mr. Davies asked, frowning thoughtfully.

"No, the manipulator," said Mrs. Davies. "The one with the red hair and braces."

Mr. Davies's expression cleared and he repressed a tiny shudder. "Oh, that girl was crazy."

"I thought Cooper preferred blondes," Gloria said.

"Right now, Cooper would prefer a prostate exam," Cooper said sourly. "Can't a guy eat his lunch before—"

"Gloria Adams?" said a woman as she approached their table. "Your office said you might be here. I told them I was your cousin."

Gloria frowned and looked more closely at the woman. A bell of recognition rang somewhere in her head, but it was muted. "Yes? Have we met?"

"Not yet," the woman said. "But I thought it was time I laid eyes on the woman who's been having an affair with my husband."

Chapter 10

Gloria went rigid with suffocating shock, as though she'd been dipped in wet concrete that was beginning to harden around her. The chattering of the café crowd fell away, leaving her excruciatingly aware of the horrified faces of Cooper and his parents, none of whom seemed any more able to speak than she was.

She gaped at the woman.

No, not the woman. Aaron's wife, whose framed vacation picture—smiling on the slopes of some mountain, with a woolly hat pulled low over her forehead and her skis standing next to her—Gloria had once seen in his office, and who had a name: Amy.

He'd talked about Amy over the years, of course, an ongoing litany about how horrible their relationship was, how they'd become roommates who shared the bills but little else and how he could never, ever want another woman, especially his wife, as much as he wanted Gloria.

That last bit was a lie, Gloria realized now. It had to be a lie.

Because the Amy standing in front of her right now, staring at her with unblinking brown eyes, wasn't the Wicked Witch of the West that Gloria had imagined her to be, and she wasn't a grandmotherly frump who wore polyester elastic pants and let her roots go gray, and she certainly wasn't a hysterical mess who created turmoil and drama wherever she went.

No.

This Amy was a slightly older, slightly taller but otherwise more beautiful version of Gloria herself. And she realized that Aaron had a type, and she and Amy were both it. The woman that Aaron was probably sleeping with now—because a man like Aaron always had a woman on the field, a woman warming up in the bull pen and a woman on the bench—would also be the same type.

They had the same small-breasted, long-legged build, same wavy black hair, same brown skin, same oval face and same almond-tipped brown eyes. Gloria had to fight hard to kill the burble of hysterical laughter that was surging its way up her throat. If someone decided to make a movie of Amy's life and put out a casting call, Gloria would get the part, no problem. No audition needed.

And just to add insult to injury, Amy was wearing a gray wrap dress that Gloria had tried on the other week at Nordstrom, then put back when she realized it made her shoulders look too boxy.

Amy's shoulders looked great in that gray dress.

Gloria opened her mouth and tried to activate her voice.

Her voice wasn't ready.

Which was crazy, because she'd thought about this moment. Mentally rehearsed this moment. Dreaded this moment. For two years she'd hurt this woman, a woman who'd never done anything to her, and the whole time Gloria had told herself it was okay because a love like she and Aaron shared could never be denied. And then, when she realized there wasn't much in Aaron that she could love, she'd told herself that at least his wife, the poor soul who was actually saddled, through marriage and their children, to the lying bastard, never knew about the affair.

Gloria had clung to the ridiculous fiction that as long as this moment never came, she hadn't truly hurt Amy.

And now, staring into Amy's brown eyes, so much like hers it was like looking into a fogged mirror, Gloria watched her rationalization go up in smoke.

Still, she tried to do the thing she'd always said she'd do—dodge and deflect. To protect this innocent woman from the painful truth.

"I beg your pardon," Gloria said coolly. Her vocal cords had dried up, producing only a brittle croak. "I don't know what you're talking about."

A humorless smile crinkled the outer edges of Amy's eyes. "Oh, I think you do."

Cooper—wonderful, loyal, strong Cooper, whose only fault, as far as Gloria could see, was that he'd developed feelings for Gloria when she wasn't remotely good enough for him—slid his chair back and stood, gently putting a hand on Amy's arm. His gaze was turbulent and worried as he glanced at Gloria, but none of that showed when he turned to Amy.

"You'd better go," he softly told her, trying to steer her away from the table. Gloria held her breath, praying it would work but knowing it wouldn't. "You've got the wrong person. Come on. I'll get you a cab."

Amy shrugged him off. All her energy was focused on Gloria. "We'd just gotten back together. Did you know that? We agreed that we needed some time apart, and then, before he could even move out, he came back and told me he'd made a mistake. He said he wants the marriage. And I want the marriage. We've been together for twenty-eight years. Since college. Did you think about that when you were climbing into bed with him?"

Gloria opened her mouth to issue another rote denial, but it felt like concrete was hardening around her throat, making it impossible to breathe, much less speak.

"No. You probably didn't," Amy continued. "But I thought you should know that things have been great in the last couple of months. Until this morning. When I was on the way to the dry cleaner's. And I found this in his suit pants."

Gloria knew what it was going to be and was already shaking her head by the time Amy reached into her bag and pulled out Aaron's secret cell phone. She should've been prepared, but seeing it in Amy's hand was still like being staked through the heart.

"It's my husband's secret cell phone," Amy told her. "And guess what's on it."

Desperation galvanized Gloria into standing up and trying one final offensive, even though she knew it was useless. "I'm sorry you're having a tough time, but I don't know what you're talking about—"

"About a thousand text messages to you." Smiling crookedly, Amy held the phone up, as though there was any possibility that Gloria wanted to examine the texts. "And his call records went crazy a couple of months ago. Looks like he was desperate to get hold of you, huh? This is you, right?" She thumbed a button and checked the display. "Gloria Adams? That's your email signature, isn't it?"

Shame now had Gloria in a choke hold. It took every ounce of her dwindling strength to hold Amy's gaze and try to look bewildered and innocent while all around them curious heads were turning in their direction.

Another chair scrape. Mr. Davies was on his feet now, dividing his concerned gaze between Amy and Gloria. "Ma'am," he tried, "let's get you to a cab. You're upset."

"I'm not upset," Amy told him.

Gloria, who was riveted by Amy's calm and dry-eyed recitation of facts, believed her. Amy wasn't upset. She just wanted the chance to say her piece.

And Gloria was no longer certain she should keep trying to stop her.

If she hadn't done right by Amy in the past, didn't she at least owe her the truth now?

"I just want Gloria to know what she's done," Amy added. "Are you her parents?" She looked at Cooper. "Her boyfriend? Then you should know what she's done, too, right?"

"Amy," Gloria said low, staring at the diamond pendant on Amy's necklace because she felt certain she'd splinter into a million crying pieces if she looked any of these people in the eye right now, "let's go outside. Please."

Amy stared at her, her face expressionless and yet oddly triumphant.

"I thought you didn't know what I was talking about." Amy arched one of her elegant brows. "So how did you know my name?"

After that, there was nowhere to go and nothing left for Gloria to say except the obvious. And she wouldn't say it through a sniveling mess of tears, either. She'd made this bed of nails, so she needed to be woman enough to lie on it. If Amy could be calm, so could she.

"I'm sorry," Gloria confessed, holding Amy's gaze. Cooper edged closer, putting a light hand on the small of Gloria's back for support. That touch may have been, out of all the moments they'd spent together in the past couple of months, the second she fell hopelessly and irrevocably in love with him. Taking a deep breath, she pressed on, aware of Mr. and Mrs. Davies discreetly slipping away from the table. "I know it's a pathetic thing to say. I know I shouldn't even be looking you in the face. I know you could never forgive me, so I'm not going to waste your time asking." She paused, hoping her tears held off for another second or two longer. "I'll never forgive myself. But I want you to know that I'm ashamed, and if I had the chance to take it all back, I would. I just… I'm sorry."

Amy stepped closer, getting up in her face but still maintaining her polite tone and smoothly blank expression. "Here's what you need to be sorry for, Gloria. You need to be sorry for making me question my marriage. Not just the time you were with my husband but the entire marriage, because now I can't figure out what was true and what wasn't true. You need to be sorry that I have to go to my doctor now and humiliate myself by asking for an HIV test—"

Gloria's chin began to quiver. She pressed her lips together, holding back a sob with difficulty. "No, you don't. We used condoms. Religiously."

"—and you need to be really sorry that I have to tell my children why I'm finally going through with the divorce. I want you to think about that. Live with it."

"I'm sorry," Gloria said helplessly. "But please don't throw it all away because of me. I'm not worth it."

"Oh, I know you're not worth it." A ghostly half smile flickered across Amy's face. "You're nothing. Which is why I want you to know that I do forgive you." That smile widened into something crooked and hard, and there, at last, was all of Amy's bottled-up emotion, flashing in her eyes. "I'm not going to eat myself up hating you. You're not worth it. So I forgive you. God will deal with you."

Yes, Gloria thought. He certainly would. She lost her battle with the tears and was forced to swipe one away as it trailed down her cheek.

Amy, mercifully, seemed to be done with her. Giving Gloria a final narrow-eyed look, she hitched her bag higher on her shoulder and turned to go. But after one step, she wheeled back around. Gloria braced for a slap across the face, which was no more than she had coming, but what Amy did was infinitely worse.

"I'm betting God's going to punish you by putting doubt in your mind." Amusement lit her expression. "I bet you're going to spend your life wondering whether this man—" she pointed to Cooper, whose face had turned to stone "—or the next man or the man after that, whichever man you love, is going to be the one to take up with a woman like you and break your heart the way you broke mine."

With that, Amy strode back through the glass doors leading to the crowded sidewalk, her head high and her spine straight, leaving a ringing silence in her wake.

After a couple of excruciating beats, the nearest diners, who hadn't bothered to pretend they weren't listening, put their heads together and began to murmur. Gloria, dumb and frozen with humiliation, stood there and wished God would finish her off with a lightning strike.

Cooper edged closer, dropping his voice. The hand on her back was hard now, as though he was as strung tight with nerves as she was.

"Gloria," he said urgently.

"Don't." She shook him off, not daring to glance anywhere near his direction because there was zero chance she could look him in the eye at this point. "Just…don't."

With another quick swipe at her eyes, she grabbed her purse, fished out her wallet and left a twenty on the table because Cooper shouldn't have to pay for her soup when she'd ruined what should have been a lovely lunch with his parents. Then, with Cooper hot on her heels, she headed for his parents, who were huddled together in the seating area near the dessert case, trying not to look as embarrassed as they surely were.

When they saw her coming, they shot to their feet. Gloria spoke quickly to spare them the further discomfort of trying to think of something to say to her. They'd had enough awkwardness in this one short trip to last a lifetime.

She didn't dare try to shake their hands again.

"I'm just going to go," she told them, knowing she'd never see them again. "It was such a pleasure to meet you."

Cooper's parents exchanged dismayed looks. Mrs. Davies hurried forward, put a hand on her arm and gave her a gentle squeeze. Staring into her kind, judgment-free eyes, Gloria had a perfect glimpse of why Cooper had turned out so well.

"Don't run off, Gloria," she told her. "You need something to eat. Come on."

"That's right." Mr. Davies took her other elbow and flashed a quick smile. "And I haven't had the chance to tell you about my race-day smoothies yet."

Standing her ground and resisting their efforts to steer her back to the table, Gloria smiled at these lovely people, who were as different from her own dysfunctional family as swans were from bats. They were kind and gracious, but they didn't truly want her around, and they sure as hell wouldn't want her dating their precious son now.

"I appreciate that, but I can't stay," Gloria said.

"Gloria." Cooper's body all but hummed with frustration. His eyes were more gray than blue now, the turbulent color of a storm rolling in on the horizon. "I'll take you home."

"No," she said firmly, hanging on to her smile and willing her tears of shame to hold off one more second—just another second!—before they fell, because another humiliation right now, no matter how tiny, would probably kill her outright. "You're going to stay here and eat with your parents because they're wonderful people."

A muscle in the back of his jaw began to tick. "I'll talk to you later, then."

Gloria stared up into his determined face for a long beat, trying to figure out whether his dogged optimism in the face of hopelessness was the best or worst thing about him.

Probably the best thing, she finally decided, giving him a sad smile.

"Goodbye, Cooper."

Chapter 11

That night, Cooper bullied the manager at Gloria's building into taking him upstairs to Gloria's door so he could check on her. He'd endured a stilted lunch with his parents, during which they'd tried to make him feel better and assured him they didn't know Gloria well enough to have formed opinions about her. Then he'd gone back to the office for an afternoon of meetings too important to reschedule. Throughout, he'd called or texted Gloria every hour or so, but the only response he'd had was radio silence. Now it was eight-ten, a time when he knew she'd be home from the hospital, and he wasn't going to let her refusal to answer the door stop him from seeing her.

She'd had all afternoon to lick her wounds, and too

much was at stake here for him to leave her to her own self-destructive devices.

"I don't think she's here, man," the beleaguered manager told him after a couple minutes of pounding. "Why not call her again?"

"She's here, and I need to make sure she's okay," Cooper snapped, running both hands through his hair in frustration and thinking hard. There was only one answer. "Open it," he said, pointing to the door.

The manager's jaw hit the floor. "I'm not opening it on your say-so—"

Cooper flashed a hundred-dollar bill in the guy's face.

Suddenly, the door swung open from the inside.

Gloria, wearing shorts and a T-shirt, her lips thinned with irritation, surveyed them and crossed her arms over her chest. Her gaze—she didn't look as if she'd been crying recently, thank God—flickered past Cooper to the building manager. Her frown deepened.

"If you take a bribe to let this man into my apartment, Roy," she snapped, "I'll have you fired. I don't care if you did give me the recipe for your mother's potato salad last Memorial Day. You got me?"

The man, who didn't appear to be fooled by her flinty-eyed glare, jerked a thumb in Cooper's direction. "You want me to throw the bum out?"

Gloria's expression softened, though she still didn't meet Cooper's eyes. "No," she told Roy. "I can take it from here." She tried to smile, but her lips didn't move much past horizontal. "Thanks."

Lobbying a final dark look in Cooper's direction, the guy left. Cooper took the opportunity to study Gloria, whose features were so resolute and hard that his relief at seeing her slipped away. This was not the face of a woman willing to listen to reason.

The knotted ball of fear inside him throbbed harder than ever.

"Hi," he said.

"Hi."

"Are you going to look at me?"

The sharpness in his tone seemed to take her by surprise. Her dark gaze flicked to his. Wary. Defiant. And, buried beneath all that, still humiliated and ashamed.

Gloria, being Gloria, tried to hide her emotions behind her bravado. "What's your problem, Cooper?"

"Can I come in?" he snapped. He had no intentions of standing out in the hall while they hashed out the future of their relationship, which was the same thing as the future of his life.

Huffing at this rudeness, she stood aside and swept him in, slamming the door behind him. He stalked into the living room, then wheeled around to face her.

"I left you a thousand messages. Thanks for letting me know you were okay."

She waved that aside as if he was a persistent fruit fly. "I wasn't in a talking mood. I'm allowed."

"I was worried. You could've sent me a text. And just so you know? Hiding and licking your wounds doesn't work for me."

Her brows hitched higher, mocking him. "Eagle Scout's got a temper."

"And Doc's a coward."

"I'm not a coward," she cried, puffing with outrage.

"And I'm not Aaron. So don't try to pull a disappearing act on me."

She blinked with shock and a new wariness.

"Believe me," she told him, "I know you're not Aaron."

"Great. Then we're on the same page."

"I doubt that." She rubbed her eyes with the heels of her hands, probably because that was the best way to avoid looking directly at him. She looked bleary and defeated. "Okay, so, you came, you saw that I'm okay, I can see that you're okay, so…we're good, right?" She headed for the door. "Have a great night. I'm tired."

"Not so fast." He leaned against the sectional's arm and crossed his ankles and arms. "I want to know what's going on in that head."

Vibrating with edginess, she paced a few steps away and came right back, ruffling her hair with her hands. "You want to do this now?" she demanded.

He felt a pulse of fear. "Right now."

"Fine." Her mouth twisted with some combination of words she couldn't force herself to say and unshed tears. Her nostrils flared. She tried to smooth her hair, tucking it behind one ear. "Fine. Here it is: I don't think this is working. So I can't see you anymore."

A smile, bitter and involuntary, stretched his lips. Could he read this woman like a large-print picture book or what?

"You're nothing if not predictable."

"What's that supposed to mean?"

"What's changed, Glo?"

She had the nerve to cock her head and look confused. "Pardon me?"

"You've been up-front with me about your relationship with that guy since practically the day we met. I know you're not a saint. I'm not a saint either. I'm okay with our mutual flaws, and I thought you were, too. So what's changed?"

She made a brittle sound, a hiccuping sob.

"What's changed is that now I know what I've done." Her voice was shrill, just this side of hysteria. "It's not emotional Monopoly money anymore, Cooper. It's real. Do you get that? What's changed is that now I've met the woman I hurt, and now I've looked her in the eyes, and now I'll have to live with the fact that she wasn't going to divorce him before, but she is now."

Now he was the one who couldn't hold her gaze. The seething pain in her eyes was more than he could take. "I know," he said quietly. "I understand. You feel guilty. You're ashamed."

"Yeah! I'm ashamed! And I was ashamed in front of your parents today, Cooper! The *one* time a guy I'm dating actually wants to introduce me to his family, my sordid past shows up to the party!"

"Look." He took a deep breath, determined to get this exactly right. "It wasn't the way I wanted it to go with them. I wanted them to see the amazing woman I see when I look at you. It wasn't good, no."

She looked slightly mollified that he understood the gravity of the situation. "The word you're looking for is *bad*, Cooper. It was *bad*."

"So we'll have to deal with that. And we will. But it's got nothing to do with our relationship, Gloria. Our relationship is solid and getting better every day."

"What?" she said on an incredulous laugh. "You didn't just say that."

"Hell, yeah, I did."

"You're not that clueless, Cooper!" Her voice rose to a shout. "I don't get to burn down someone's house over here, and then come over here and build myself a beautiful new house to live in! It doesn't work that way! I should get nothing! That's how it works!"

"You're doing it to yourself!" he yelled back. "My feelings haven't changed! I'm not trying to punish you!"

"You should be," she said quietly, her shoulders drooping. "And you would be. If you'd stop letting your hormones do the thinking for you."

He stared her down until some of her defiance wavered and fell.

"That was beneath you."

"It's true," she insisted.

Frustration made his entire body seize up, all the way down to his fists.

"It's not true! You think I'm not capable of figuring out when I care about someone versus when I just want to screw them? Really? Is that what you think of me?"

"No." She gave him a gentle smile—a sad, tender

smile—and that was the moment he realized that this battle was 90 percent lost, and unless a team of SEALs was on its way to help him out, he wasn't going to win. "No. I think that when you calm down and think about it, you'll know I'm right." She paused, her smile fading. "I can't stand to look at myself in the mirror. Why would you think I'm a good candidate for a relationship with you?"

He was up against a brick wall, clearly, but he couldn't just let her go. Not Gloria. His desperation level hit the red zone, making it impossible for him to think clearly before choosing his words. Not that he had any explanation for the certainty he'd felt the second he laid eyes on her that she was…that she was…

"Because you are a good candidate," he said flatly.

"That's crazy talk, Cooper!"

"What do you want me to say?" he roared. "I can't describe it in terms that make sense! It's *you,* Gloria! It's always been you! It's, I don't know, it's the look in your eyes, like you're Wonder Woman and this lost little girl, all rolled up in one." She stilled, frowning. "It's your bravado. It's your incredible brain. It's your killer instinct. You'd rather chew gravel than lose to anyone at anything." She blinked, opening her mouth and then closing it again. "It's your face. It's your body. It's because you watch *Doctor Who* and know who all the villains are. It's the way you take such good care of your sister, and you never even think you should look out for yourself like that. It's the way you look at me when you think I don't notice."

Her face was bright red now, her eyes shining

but still sad. She pressed her hands to her cheeks as though checking for a fever, and then lowered one to cover her heart.

They stared at each other.

"You're not going to make this easy, are you?" she said.

"Fuck easy."

She almost smiled at that, but she didn't swerve one inch off her path.

"It shouldn't be me." She was all quiet patience, the way a kindergarten teacher demonstrates proper shoe-tying techniques to her class. "You want someone you can be proud of with your parents. A good person. Someone better than me."

"Don't you get it?" he asked tiredly. "There is no one better than you. Not for me."

Gloria, damn her, stood there watching with those dispassionate eyes, hearing but not believing. He wondered what he could ever say or do that would make her believe.

She smiled benevolently at him. "There will be someone better. You'll thank me for this one day. You'll see."

That was when he lost it. Big-time.

"Screw you!" he thundered. "You don't get to stand there ruining my life and act like you're giving me the winning lottery ticket! You don't get to throw us away! You don't get to decide who's right for me and who's not! Half of this is about what I want, Gloria! It's not all about you!"

Defiant to the soles of her feet, Gloria glared at him, her chin hitched up.

And then, quite suddenly, she fell apart.

With a shrill cry...a choked sob...a twisted, ruined face...she lashed out at him, planting both palms on his chest and pushing so hard he staggered back several steps.

"You can't do this to me!" she shrieked. "Why can't you see that I ruin things? I don't want to ruin you!"

"Gloria." Alarmed, he reached for her. "It's okay—"

"It's not okay!" She was sobbing now, barely able to get the words out. "You have to leave. You have to leave, Cooper!"

"I'm not leaving you!"

Another shove, harder this time. "Go! You think I want you to see me falling apart like this? Leave!"

Hiccupping herself into silence, this proud, stubborn woman crossed her arms over her chest and took a shuddering breath. How she managed it, he had no idea, but when she spoke again, her voice was hoarse but calm.

"Please, Cooper." Crossing to the door, she opened it for him and waited.

He stood there, paralyzed with fear and unable to make his feet move out of the apartment. If he left, how would he ever get back in again? But on the other hand, this wasn't only about what he needed. Right now Gloria needed space, and he was, and always would be, all about giving her what she needed.

So, doing his best impersonation of a full-grown man rather than the primitive mass of emptiness and fear he felt like, he followed her but lingered on the threshold.

"Look at me." His voice was husky. Urgent.

Nostrils flaring, she pointedly turned her head in the other direction and refused to meet his gaze.

This rejection was like another piece of his heart sliced off and mashed beneath her foot. Swallowing the tight knot in his throat, he plowed ahead.

"Send me away," he said, shrugging. "It doesn't matter. I'm here." He touched a finger to her temple. She flinched. "And I'm here," he continued, touching her chest and feeling, for one quick second, the runaway thump of her heart. "And we both know it. Don't we?"

At that, her gaze flickered back to him, vulnerable and raw.

He wanted to stay.

The hardest thing he ever did was turn and walk away.

Chapter 12

Three Months Later

Gloria stared at herself in the full-length mirror at the bridal boutique, seeing nothing. All her energy was tied up with her thoughts, which swirled and fluttered like fall leaves before a storm, resisting all her efforts to rake them into a manageable pile.

This was it. Zero hour.

After months of planning and anticipation, Talia and Tony's wedding weekend had arrived.

Cooper would be there this weekend, of course; the chances of him missing his cousin Tony's wedding were nonexistent. So she'd see him as early as tomorrow, depending on which flight he'd booked.

Hell, for all she knew, they'd be sitting next to each

other for the long flight to Bora-Bora, and wouldn't that be fun? Not. It would be awkward. Uncomfortable. Excruciating.

They hadn't laid eyes on each other since the day she fell apart and kicked him out. A day that had the distinction of being the very worst day of her life, other than the days her parents had died.

The worst non-death day of her life.

He'd called and texted; she'd evaded.

Would he bring someone? Yeah, he probably would, because what red-blooded male wanted to spend a long weekend in a lush tropical paradise without a warm female body? What would she do if he did bring someone? Collapse in a sobbing heap on the beach? Faint? Die? No, she thought grimly. Her pride had been gravely wounded, but it wasn't gone. No. If and when she saw Cooper or his new squeeze this weekend, she planned to play it cool and collected.

Oh, Cooper, hi, she'd say. Or, *Cooper! It's great to see you again.*

Something breezy and nonchalant.

Something that hid the fact that she'd turned into a zombie—all walking shell, with little to no humanity left on the inside—in the months since she'd last seen him.

"Oh, Gloria," sighed an exasperated voice. "Will you please eat a cookie? What the hell are you doing to yourself?"

Gloria snapped out of her thoughts.

"What?" she asked vaguely, looking around. "What is it—? Oh, Tally, you look gorgeous!"

Talia, who stood on the platform next to Gloria's in the fitting room at the high-end bridal boutique where Talia had found her gown, had her arms crossed and was glowering at Gloria but otherwise looked amazing. She'd chosen an ivory chiffon Grecian goddess gown that draped over one shoulder and was so light and airy she'd probably float down to the beachfront chapel without her feet ever touching the ground. The sheer veil had floral lace trim and, because Talia was an artist who never did anything without a pop of color, her sash, sandals and decorative comb were all in a vivid shade of blue-green called Pacific Paradise.

Gloria was speechless. If there'd ever been a more beautiful bride than Talia or a bride more deserving of a perfect wedding day in the perfect setting, she couldn't think who.

"Oh, Tally." Gloria pressed a hand to her heart and gave herself a stern warning to stop cooing before she teared up and started dripping black mascara, an offense that would probably warrant banishment from the pristine elegance of this designer boutique. "I'm so happy for you. I can't believe you're getting married in three days. What happened to my annoying baby sister?"

"Funny you should say that." Talia's frown deepened, grooving down her forehead and between her eyes. "I'm wondering what's happening to you! You're wasting away! You get thinner every time I see you, so don't bother denying it again."

"I don't know what you're talking about," Gloria lied.

"Look at you," Talia said, flapping a hand at the angled mirrors ringing the platforms. "You're down a good ten pounds. Maybe fifteen. I'm not blind."

The two salon owners, also sisters, nodded with grim agreement. One knelt at Talia's feet and fussed with her hem, and the other frowned as she stood behind Gloria and tugged at the loose bodice of her maid-of-honor dress, a knee-length chiffon halter number, also in Pacific Paradise. They'd taken a special interest in Talia's wedding when they heard about her battle with Hodgkin's disease, and they'd all become very friendly.

"This hangs on you like you got it from a Liz Taylor yard sale, Gloria," said the younger co-owner, Becky, darkly. "Why not just wear a sheet and be done with it? Why bother with this?" She flapped a hand to indicate the overpriced salon in all its glittering, chandelier-lit glory.

"Excuse me." Gloria stepped away from Becky's grasping hands and tried to adjust the cups over her now-nonexistent bosom. When that effort failed, she put her hands on her hips and worked on looking dignified. "But since when is being thin a problem for you fashion folks here on Madison Avenue?"

"Since your scrawny little shoulders are the only thing keeping the gown from sliding to the floor in a wrinkled heap," said the other owner, Helga, heaving herself to her feet and coming over to join Becky as they fidgeted with Gloria's dress. "You're not sick, too, are you? Because Talia's the picture of health now that she's finished with her treatments, and you, meanwhile, look terrible. Are you sick? You're sick, aren't you?"

"No," Gloria said shortly.

Becky and Helga stared at Gloria in the mirror, one over each shoulder, and shook their heads with disapproving concern. And then a lightbulb seemed to go off over Helga's head.

"Man trouble." She nodded wisely. "That's what it is. You've got a broken heart. You're sick with it."

"I am not—"

"Trust me." Another nod from Helga. "I know a broken heart from sick. Not to worry, though. I know someone. You'll love him. It won't be perfect, mind you. He's not black, but at your age? I wouldn't be too picky."

This was their fourth trip to the salon for shopping and fittings, so Gloria had gotten used to liberal doses of free advice, which usually ran to topics like where to find the freshest seafood and which Broadway shows everyone must see before they died. But this was too much, even from Helga.

Irritated, Gloria caught Talia's eye in the mirror before stepping out of her teetering heels and climbing down from the platform. Then she stalked over to the seating area, plopped down on the silk sofa and took a healthy sip of champagne from her fizzing flute.

"Is this why the dresses are so expensive? Buy a dress and you get matchmaking advice and a beaded bag to go with?"

"Calm down, Glo," said Talia, always the peacemaker.

Helga, meanwhile, was also getting a little huffy. "Well, pardon me for noticing how pale you are," she said. "Pardon me for wondering if you're coming down with something with bags like that under your eyes. I'll never mention it again. We won't speak of it."

"Great," said Gloria, finishing the rest of her champagne.

"Even though I've married off four daughters," Helga continued, pouting now. "Even though three of them married doctors. Forget it. What do I know?"

"Four and a half," corrected Becky. "Because you introduced my Julie to her husband."

"Yeah, but they got divorced." Helga paused. "So we'll call it four and a quarter. Anyway. No matter." Lobbing a final glare at Gloria, she turned her attention back to the bride. "Talia, your dress is ready now. We'll get it packed up for the flight. Gloria, Becky will have to take yours in again, so you'll have to come back tomorrow."

"Fine." Gloria, who had by now grabbed the champagne bottle from the bucket, topped off her glass and drunk it down again, was just buzzed enough to start blabbing. "If you must know, I had an affair with a married man. And then I had a rough breakup, and I'm having a tough time getting over it. I haven't been that hungry. So I've lost a little weight. The end."

"See?" asked Helga. "Was that so hard?"

Repressing a snort, Gloria planted her elbow on the back of the sofa and rested her chin on her hand. Then she decided more liquid courage would make this conversation go down a whole lot easier.

"Well, there you go." Helga wagged a finger at Gloria. "You should be counting your lucky stars that cheating son of a bitch is out of your life. He'd have a new mistress before the ink was dry on your marriage license. You'd never know a moment's peace without wondering—"

"Not him!" Gloria was in the process of refilling her glass when Talia stomped over, snatched the bottle from her and plopped it back into the bucket with a swish of ice water. Gloria gave her a sharp smack on the butt. "I was dating someone new."

"Oh?" Helga asked, brows raised.

"But it didn't work out."

"Why?" asked Becky.

"Yes, Glo." Talia poured herself a glass of champagne, sat next to Gloria on the sofa and fixed her with a gaze that was unrelenting and disapproving. "Tell us all why you can't be with Cooper, a good man who was crazy about you and good for you. Tell us why you're insisting on martyrdom—"

Gloria couldn't believe her ears. *"Martyrdom?"*

"—even though you've been doing all sorts of good deeds, like donating your time to the clinic that treats kids with cleft palates—"

"Nice," said Becky, exchanging approving nods with Helga.

"—and sending an apology letter to Aaron's wife."

"Did she read it?" Helga asked, wide-eyed.

"I don't know," Gloria admitted.

"The point is, Glo, that there's nothing more you can possibly do to make up for the past," Talia concluded. "So, please. Tell us why you can't be with Cooper. And go slowly and use small words so I'll understand this time."

"This is why I never tell you anything," Gloria snapped. "You judge me. You're always judging me. You judged me for staying with Aaron, and now you're judging me for breaking up with Cooper. There's no pleasing you."

"Oh, bullshit," said Talia. "Don't you dare—"

"Ladies, please." Becky clapped her hands. "No swearing around the gowns. They're sensitive. We don't want them to absorb negative energy."

Gloria and Talia shot guilty looks at the rows of gorgeous gowns.

"Sorry," Talia muttered.

"In fact, bride-to-be, you take that dress off right now before you wrinkle it or dribble champagne on it," Becky commanded.

"Yes, ma'am," Talia said meekly, putting down her glass and scurrying behind the dressing screen to change.

"And you two argue on your own time." Helga slung her tape measure around her neck, helped herself to Talia's glass and perched on the sofa's arm. "Right now I'm trying to understand the situation. You say he was a good man?"

"Yes," Gloria admitted.

"Handsome? With a job? A *good* job?" Helga went on.

"Yes," said Gloria.

"Kind to women and small animals? Not gay?"

"Correct."

"What about his mother?" Helga seemed to be holding her breath as she waited for the answer to this most important question. "Is he a good son? Does he take good care of his mother?"

"Yes," Gloria said.

Helga clapped a hand to her forehead. "Well, it's like you found a live unicorn prancing around in Grand Central Terminal!" she cried. "What's the problem, for crying out loud?"

Gloria dropped her gaze the way she always did when this shameful episode came up. Then, in a valiant effort at laying all her cards on the table, she opened her mouth but discovered at the very last second that she couldn't get the words out. It sounded so overwrought to say that she wasn't good enough for Cooper or that he deserved a woman who hadn't left such a destructive trail behind her. In the end, all she could do was shut her mouth again, cross her legs and arms and wish she could disappear.

"Is it because you're afraid to tell him about your... indiscretion?" Becky asked.

"He already knows."

"So I repeat, what's the problem?" Helga interjected.

When Gloria floundered again, Talia reappeared, now dressed in her street clothes. "It's because she thinks she's not good enough for him," she said, resuming her seat and giving Gloria's shoulder a supportive squeeze. "Our father really screwed with her head. He was a doctor, too."

"Wait, what?" Gloria twisted to stare at Talia. "What're you talking about? What's Daddy got to do with this?"

Talia scowled at her. "We've talked about this before, Glo."

Gloria blinked, feeling as though her head had been clanged between a pair of cymbals. "We've never talked about Daddy and Cooper—"

"Maybe not," Talia said, shrugging, "but we've talked about how everything you do is a reaction to him walking out on the family."

"Oh," said Becky, nodding sagely. "I understand now."

"Well, I don't understand," Gloria told them all before focusing on Talia. "We've talked about how I'm an overachieving type-A doctor and that's probably a result of me trying to be a good kid so Daddy would come back home. So what? Big deal. That's the story of every divorce."

"You became a doctor because Daddy was a doctor," Talia told her. "And then you married the wrong man—one of your med school instructors, also a doctor—because of Daddy."

"I did not…" Gloria began, trailing off when the truth began to pierce the outer layer of her bravado. She hardly ever thought about her ex-husband anymore. Could Talia be right?

"Let me guess," Helga said. "Older man? Looked like your father?"

Talia pointed to Helga with one finger and touched the tip of her own nose with the other.

They all turned their heads to stare at Gloria.

Gloria got to her feet and paced away from the sofa, suddenly fidgety. Why was it so hot in here?

"Every man you've ever dated is similar to Daddy in some way, Glo. Either looks or personality. Except for Cooper."

"And the married man?" Becky asked eagerly. "How was he similar?"

"He was a cheater," Talia explained. "Just like our father. I've tried to tell her. I think she's in denial."

Helga and Becky both nodded and murmured a chorus of agreement that made Gloria feel as though she was the screwed-up guest being analyzed by a panel of experts on a TV shrink's show.

"And daughters of cheaters often turn into the other women," Helga said. "Everybody knows that. It's a pattern. You don't want to be the victim like your mother was, so you turn into the perpetrator instead." She waved an airy hand. "Classic situation."

"I know," Talia said sadly. "And she never even gave Cooper a real chance."

Gloria, who'd now paced her way to the farthest corner of the seating area, frowned and stared at the fringed rug beneath her bare feet. Her brain was so full of explosive new ideas it felt as if it might blow off her head at any second.

Maybe she *had* been in denial all this time.

Talia's analysis had never made this much sense before. Or maybe Gloria had never been ready to listen before.

"This Cooper," Helga said. "He sounds like a good guy, eh, Gloria?"

Gloria was filled with a sudden ache of longing for him so powerful she couldn't answer.

"Gloria?" Helga raised her voice and snapped her fingers several times. "Stop daydreaming and get back over here. We're talking to you."

"Leave her alone," Talia said firmly. "She needs a minute to think and remember what I always tell her."

"And what's that?" asked Becky.

"Life's short," Talia said. "Anyone can get sick at any time. So there's no time to let emotional bullshit keep you from being happy."

Chapter 13

Bora-Bora, Gloria decided two days later, was the most beautiful paradise God ever created, and well worth the hellish sixteen-hour flight plus the additional flight from Tahiti it took to get there. True, she had no idea what day it was, much less the current time, and she was both wired and exhausted, but she'd find a way to cope. It was far better to be wired and exhausted with a turquoise lagoon in front of you and lushly green Mount Otemanu rising in the distance behind you than it was to be wired and exhausted as she usually was, coming off a long day in the operating room.

She, Talia, Tony and most of the Davies relatives had arrived a little while ago and checked into the high-end resort. Since they had several hours until the rehearsal dinner, she'd showered and unpacked. Now, with time to kill, she stepped out of her bungalow and rested her elbows on the porch rail, breathing in the tangy sea air laced with the fragrance of frangipani, jasmine and dozens of other flowers whose names she would never know. The sun shone, the breeze ruffled her hair, and—honest to God—there was even a rainbow arching down from the mountain to the leafy valley below.

And the lagoon…

The bungalows, welcoming and quaint with their thatched roofs and wooden walkways in between, sat on stilts atop the bluest ocean she'd ever seen. Actually, blue didn't begin to describe it. Patches of the sparkling water were turquoise, but others were indigo…sapphire…aquamarine… She didn't know the names for all the colors of blue that extended for as far as her squinting eyes could see, but she could happily stand there forever trying to figure it out. True, the tropical sun would roast her bare shoulders like the rehearsal-dinner pig currently turning on the spit back at the resort's main house, but that would be a small price to pay for getting to spend time in this kind of natural beauty.

Breathing deep, she sighed and wondered how her poor lungs would ever readjust to smoggy Manhattan air after this.

Cooper hadn't been on her flight, which meant that if he'd arrived already, she hadn't seen him yet. Which was probably just as well, because she hadn't figured out what she'd say to him when she saw him again.

The whole thing with Talia, Becky and Helga at the fitting had really thrown her for a loop, and she hadn't recovered yet. That was the problem with the truth: too often, she knew it when she heard it. And, man, had she heard it or what?

So what were her lessons?

She gave that some hard thought, brushing her fluttering hair out of her eyes and trying to arrange her thoughts into some semblance of order.

The biggest one, she supposed, was that she reacted to men based upon her experiences with her father. Most recently, she'd hooked up with Aaron because he was like her father. A charming and successful doctor, darkly handsome with an easy smile for any pretty woman and a voice as smooth and deep as bittersweet chocolate. And if that was true, didn't it also mean that she'd pushed Cooper away because he wasn't like her father? In addition to the obvious physical differences, he was giving and open, with, as far as she could tell, no hidden agendas, games or tricks up his sleeves.

He showed up when he was supposed to, which meant he wanted to be with her. There'd been no disappearing acts with Cooper, no tortured explanations that began with, *See, baby, what had happened was...* He listened to her and was responsive to her wishes, even when they didn't coincide with his. He laughed with her; he comforted her; he scorched her with a single blue-eyed look. He'd introduced her to his parents.

He...scared her.

That was really the bottom line, wasn't it?

The truly good guys in the world had thus far made it a practice to stay far away from her. Why would this one—who knew everything about her—actually want her?

Didn't *that* have to be a trick?

Wasn't there an *April Fool's!* lurking out there in her immediate future if she went back to Cooper?

"Gloria? Is that you?"

Startled, she straightened and wheeled around to discover a couple coming down the walkway nearest hers, but she didn't recognize the woman's voice and the sun was behind them, obscuring their features. Shielding her eyes with her hand, she looked again and discovered—

Oh, God. It was Mr. and Mrs. Davies.

Cooper's parents! She froze, her mouth drying out.

"Gloria!" Mrs. Davies hurried forward and folded her into a bear hug. "I was hoping we'd see you today! How was your flight?"

"Umm…"

Gloria's brain stalled out. She'd known she'd see all the Davies clan here for the wedding, but she'd expected a cooler greeting from these two—something along the lines of a narrow-eyed glare or a cold shoulder. She had not expected this open delight, as though Gloria had brought the party with her.

And then, a long beat or two into the hug, it occurred to her that Mrs. Davies, a very special woman who'd raised a very special son, was going out of her way to make Gloria feel comfortable and welcome. And there was only one appropriate response to that.

Gloria burst into tears.

And hugged her back.

"Look what you did," Mr. Davies told his wife. "You made the woman cry. Why don't you let her go before you drive her to jump off the walkway and drown herself in the water? Come here, Gloria. It's okay."

"I'm sorry." Laughing now, Gloria gave Mr. Davies a quick hug and dabbed her eyes with the linen handkerchief he fished out of his back pocket for her. "I didn't mean to cry on you. And I'm so sorry for the whole scene at the restaurant. You must think I'm a—"

"We don't think anything." Mrs. Davies held Gloria's forearms in her firm grip. She looked over her shoulder at her husband. "Do we think anything?"

"No," Mr. Davies said flatly. "Now that I'm retired, I never think when I can help it."

"Cooper's a grown man," Mrs. Davies told her. "He knows how to judge people without us telling him what to do. If he likes you, then there's a reason. If Cooper has a reason, then that's reason enough for us. End of story."

Gloria laughed and cried again, ducking her head and dabbing at her eyes, which were probably a tarry black mess by now. "You're such good people. I can see why Cooper turned out so well."

"Cooper's not doing too well at the moment, Glo," Mr. Davies said, a frown marring his forehead. "He's in a world of hurt. Like a bear that's got his paw stuck in a trap. Are you going to put him out of his misery anytime soon?"

"That's his bungalow right there." Mrs. Davies pointed to the one on the other side of theirs. "He's unpacking before the rehearsal dinner."

Gloria hesitated, pressing a hand to her heart, which had gone haywire with the news that Cooper was so close. This was all too much to hope for. She had to force herself to remember to breathe. It was one thing for them not to hold the restaurant scene against her. It was something else again for them to conclude that she was a woman worthy of their precious son.

"Unless…" Mrs. Davies's face darkened "…you don't love him after all…?"

There it was, on the table for all the world to see.

Even Gloria.

"I love him," she admitted, the sudden certainty a sweet ache in her heart. "What kind of fool wouldn't?"

"Whew." Mrs. Davies wiped a hand over her forehead. "Okay, then. Now, remember—wounded bear. They snarl. They bite. They slash with their paws. You've got to wait all that out. Got it?"

"Got it. Sounds like you've had some experience with wounded bears over the years, Mrs. Davies."

Mrs. Davies nodded, but Mr. Davies pulled a frown.

"Who else do you know that acts like a wounded bear?" he asked his wife seriously.

When Gloria raised her hand to knock on the door of Cooper's bungalow a few minutes later, she discovered that her hands were shaking. Which only made sense. Her happiness was on the line here, and she had no strategy, no idea what to say and no escape plan if things went south. With her luck, Cooper would tell her to go to hell, and she'd still have to spend most of the next few days in close contact with him.

And wouldn't that be fun?

No answer at the door.

She knocked again, harder this time.

Still no answer.

Maybe he'd slipped out without his parents noticing, she thought, staring down the path to the main lodge. Or he could've gone to the pool. Maybe she could catch him there.

Without warning, the door swung open, and there he was.

Her throat tightened down as she tilted her head back to meet his gaze. It was a jolt, seeing him again. A painful jolt and, simultaneously, the best thing that could possibly happen to her. She'd forgotten how tall he was...how big...how bright his blue eyes were, as though they'd been scooped from the lagoon's tranquil waters.

Expressionless, he stared at her, his breath audibly catching in his throat.

She opened her mouth, eager to cross the divide between them. Too bad she had no idea what words to string together to get her to the other side.

He looked different. His cheeks had hollowed out, giving him a surly look that was all harsh angles and unforgiving lines. Beneath his eyes, dark smudges had appeared, as though he hadn't slept any better than she had recently.

It was as though he'd captured her misery and smeared it across his own face so he could reflect it back to her. Why had she pushed him away? To punish herself? What a masochistic idiot she was. For her, she now knew, there was no worse fate than cutting Cooper, the other, better half of herself, out of her life.

Yeah.

She definitely loved him.

His eyes narrowed, glinting now, and she knew the divide between them wasn't getting any smaller the longer she stood here.

Start talking, girl.

"Hi," she said, her voice breathy. God, she was a mess. Realizing that her raw nerves were making her link and unlink her fingers, she pulled her hands apart and stuck them in her pockets. "It's so good to see you."

No reaction other than his hard stare.

And then, without warning, his face contracted into a snarl of rage.

"Cooper," she began, alarmed.

Stepping back, he slammed the door in her face.

For one stunned and stupid second, she stared at the spot where he'd just been, wondering if he'd rip her limb from limb if she so much as tried to knock on his door again. But then she decided, *Screw it.* What was he going to do? Yell at her? Have security escort her out? Throw her into the lagoon?

Any of those possible fates were no worse than the hell of loneliness she'd been through in their time apart. She was a big girl. She could endure yelling. She had it coming.

Taking a fortifying breath, she opened the door and strode into his bungalow.

He was on her in an instant, a hulking figure emerging from the shadows cast by the plantation blinds, vibrating with suppressed fury.

"I'm trying to stay calm." Leaning down in her face, he spoke in a low rumble that was like the approaching roar of a tornado. "But I want you out of here. Now."

"We need to talk," she said, standing her ground, just as calm.

"There's nothing to say."

She shrugged. "I disagree."

For one arrested second, he gaped at her as though he couldn't believe his ears.

Then he lost it.

"Get out!" His bellowing fury broke over her like a seventy-foot wave obliterating everything in its path. The Cooper she'd known disappeared inside flashing eyes, a sneering mouth and waving hands. "You think you get to show up here and look at me with those eyes and everything's okay? Is that what you think? Huh?"

She watched him, knowing he'd never hit her but thinking anything would be better than the seething hatred in his eyes right now. But he didn't really hate her, she reminded herself, putting all her energy into not running away or, worse, cowering before him. He loved her, and he was a wounded bear right now. It was her job to stay calm and get through to him.

"I think that pushing you away was the most self-destructive thing I've ever done," she said softly. "And that's saying a lot. And I'm hoping you'll give me another chance."

This baring of her naked heart had absolutely no effect on him whatsoever.

Making a derisive sound that was a million times worse than a disbelieving snort, he grabbed her upper arm in his grip and frog-marched her back to the door.

"Get out," he said, opening it for her with his free hand. "Leave."

Jerking free, she decided to take the offensive. Getting up in his face and staring down his flashing gaze, she planted her feet and squared her shoulders. "If you want me out of here, you'll have to throw me in the lagoon."

He stilled, his breath a harsh rasp in the silence.

"And once I climb out of the water and dry myself off, I'll be right back here, asking you for another chance, and you'll have to deal with me then."

He looked away, his face twisting with some emotion she couldn't read.

"So let me know what you want to do. If it's the lagoon, I need to take off my shoes first because they were pretty expensive."

His gaze flickered back to her, and there was a lot less anger in it this time and a lot more turbulent uncertainty.

Swinging the door shut again, he stalked away toward the bed. "You have ten seconds," he said without bothering to face her. "Start talking."

Chapter 14

Predictably, all her racing thoughts chose that moment to leave her head. And there was no way she could think when he had his shoulders squared against her.

"Are you going to look at me?" she asked.

For a while it seemed as if his stony silence was the only answer she was going to get, but then he surprised her. Turning around, he ducked his head and touched his thumb and forefinger to the inside corners of his eyes. She waited, every beat of her heart a painful thud against her breastbone. Finally, he looked up, nostrils flaring and lips curling, but his focus latched on to some fixed point above her head and showed no signs of lowering.

"Five seconds," he said.

"Fine," she snapped. "You scare me."

His bloodshot gaze snapped to her face. "What?"

She hesitated, trying to get the words to match up with the way her heart swelled when she looked at him. "The way you make me feel...the way you look at me like I'm the most important person in the universe...the kind of man you are, a really good person, it just—"

"I'm a real person!" he roared. She winced, startled by this second explosion. "I'm not some idealized version of a Boy Scout you saw in a picture. I'm not a saint. I will disappoint you sooner or later—"

"You think I don't know that?"

"I'm not sure what you know. You haven't stuck around long enough to find out much about me, one way or the other. Have you?"

That stung. "I know you're an impatient neat freak and workaholic who watches way too much *Doctor Who* and has a competitive streak a mile wide," she said defensively. "I know you're a hopeless optimist even when the world isn't giving you much to be optimistic about. I know you believe in second chances, and you get all moody and sulky when you're thinking too hard. You don't say much when silence will do, but when you do talk, it's always worth listening to. I know you're a devoted brother and son. How'm I doing so far?"

She'd been looking down at her hands, counting off her points on her fingers, so it was a big surprise to look up and see that his face had gone the livid red of a lobster and his eyes were glazed with tears. His chin quivered.

"Cooper," she began, moving toward him, needing to touch him when he was in this kind of pain.

But he was beyond listening. "I gave you my heart," he shouted, balling up his fist and thumping his chest for emphasis. "Do you think I do that every day to whatever woman rolls up in a pair of heels and a little black dress? I gave you my heart, and you couldn't walk away from me fast enough! I gave you my heart—"

Galvanized by some primal instinct buried inside her, she hurried forward, reached up and cupped his hard, bristly cheeks between her hands. He stiffened, trying to jerk away, but she held him tight, sinking her fingers into his silky curls until she felt the warmth of his scalp underneath.

"Shhh." She pressed her face to the side of his, tasting the salty wetness of his tears as she spoke and reveling in the way his big body radiated heat. "Shhh," she murmured again, massaging his head, and some of the tension began to ease out of his muscles. "I'm not letting you go, so you need to stop fighting me."

Calmer now, his breath an uneven rasp, he planted his hands on her hips and brought her closer, anchoring her against him. His long-lashed gaze flicked up to hers, filling her entire field of vision with eyes that were now the deep indigo of the waters outside.

"Tell me what you want." They were so close and his voice was so low that it was as if the sound vibrated into her body. "I need to hear it."

In answer she took one of his hands and pressed it between her breasts, directly over the spot where her heart was trying to pound its way through her chest wall.

"I'm giving you my heart," she told him, unblinking. "So you'd better take good care of it."

He stiffened again, his eyes squeezing closed and his head tilting back, and for one heart-stopping second she feared she'd said the exact wrong thing. But then his lids snapped open again and he smiled a glorious smile—a smile so full of joyous relief—that it was more blindingly beautiful than anything she'd seen on this island paradise.

And then, just as quickly, his smile gave way to a look of intense determination. She suddenly couldn't breathe because the air was stuck tight in her throat. That hand of his slid away from her heart, skimming across the tip of her breast—gently scraping her nipple with his nails—on its way back to her hip. She gasped and clung to his neck, electric sensation sparking to every corner of her body. Then his hands eased around her back and drifted lower, to her ass, pressing her up against the hard length of his erection. He thrust his hips, creating the perfect friction against her sweet spot, and she went breathless with desire.

"Cooper."

"I've waited a long time for this," he murmured against her mouth, teasing by not kissing her. His fingers, meanwhile, went to work on the filmy skirt of her sundress, inching it up with painstaking care until she felt cool air against the backs of her thighs. "So if you're not sure about that, now's your chance to say so."

"I'm sure."

"Sure about what?" he asked conversationally, his hands now sliding into her panties. "That you love me?"

"Yes," she breathed, lost in the thrill of his bare skin gliding over her.

"If you love me," he said, easing her panties down and letting them drop so she could step out of them, "why haven't you said it?"

It was awfully hard to talk when she was dizzy with lust. Her hips had begun to circle of their own accord, thrusting against him, and his long fingers were rubbing her from behind, sliding back and forth in the slick cleft between her thighs.

"Because I'm scared," she admitted softly.

His fingers stilled. The delay nearly undid her, but he wanted her full attention and seemed determined not to continue until he got it. Stooping so he could look her in the face, he smiled just enough to make those sexy lines fan out from the corners of his eyes.

"And what's there for you to be scared of when it comes to you and me, Gloria?"

She hesitated, but there was only one answer, and it came straight from her heart.

"Nothing."

That seemed to please him, because her reward was swift. "Not one damn thing," he agreed, licking his way deep into her mouth and absorbing her helpless mewls of pleasure. At the same time, his talented fingers resumed their stroking from behind and, slick with her juices, glided over her core.

She shattered with a sharp, surprised cry, tensing and arching with ecstasy until only his strong arm across the small of her back kept her from collapsing to the floor. He rubbed her again and again, wringing every glittering ounce of pleasure from her until it seemed likely she would die from it. When her head fell back and her melting bones refused to support her for another second, he swept her into his arms, took a couple of steps and swung her around, ripping the linens out of the way before lowering her to the bed.

Drained yet energized, she let her heavy arms rest over her head as he loomed over her, propping one knee on the edge of the bed.

Panting slightly, she tried to catch her breath but couldn't with him staring at her with such raw intensity. His gaze touched her calves and her thighs, which were barely covered by her skirt…the front of her dress, where the decorative buttons strained against her heaving chest…her mouth and eyes.

And then, when he'd inventoried every part of her, he reached for her skirt. Taking all the time in the world, he pinched it between his fingers, easing it up until it whispered past her engorged sex, teasing her. He gave her a possessive look, his expression dark with purpose, and then leaned down, coming closer.

His tongue dipped into her belly button.

Her body spasmed. "Cooper, please."

Begging, it turned out, had no effect on him. The moment stretched between them, lasting until her overheated body began to writhe of its own accord, needing him inside her more than it needed oxygen or water. When he was close enough to smell her desire—when he had to be saturated with it—his gaze flicked up the length of her body again, to her eyes.

"This belongs to me." Bowing his head and brushing his lips across her, finding the most perfectly exquisite spot of her oversensitized flesh, he gave her a lingering kiss that made her cry out again. "You know that, right?"

The smug triumph in his expression made her want to deny it, but on the other hand, it wasn't as if she was any good at hiding her feelings for him.

"All of me belongs to you," she said softly, reaching for him. "Come here so I can show you."

The arrogance slipped off his face, replaced by urgent need. Reaching for the hem of his black T-shirt, he swept it over his head and let it drop to the floor. His jade dragon pendant was a flash of green between his collarbones. She stared at his ripped shoulders, torso and arms, dusted with a light covering of hair, smoothly tanned and glowing with health. She wondered what had made her deny herself the thrilling experience of making love with this man at the first possible opportunity.

She laughed.

Frowning, he went to work on his belt and zipper. *"What?"*

"I'm the world's biggest fool for not grabbing on to you the first chance I got, Eagle Scout."

"Yeah, I know," he said, dimpling at her. "That's why I plan to marry you before you make any other crazy mistakes."

She stared at him, not sure whether he was joking or not, and afraid to ask. The M-word, coming out of his mouth, evoked such a strong visceral yearning inside her it couldn't be ignored. What would it be like to be married to this man? To wake up to his open smile every morning and fall asleep curled up against his strong body every night? He was such a neat freak there'd be no picking his socks up off the floor; she knew that much, and they'd argue because they both had big personalities.

It would be an adventure, as everything with Cooper was.

Marriage wasn't something she'd thought about with him, largely because they'd spent so much time working out the basics of their relationship. But now that he'd said it, the possibility of it filled her from top to bottom, as though she'd swallowed a thousand glittering fireflies.

She wanted it. Oh, man, she wanted it.

"Don't play," she said.

Nothing outwardly changed in his expression, but some inner light seemed to glow brighter, making him look happier than she'd ever seen. "I'd never joke about something like that."

Unsettled, she decided to focus on what they'd been

about to do. "Why don't you stop talking and come here?"

"If you insist."

Watching her the whole time, he eased his board shorts and gray boxer briefs down, freeing an erection that was long and thick.

Watching him, she shifted restlessly, unable to keep her body still.

He climbed onto all fours and crawled up the length of her body, kneeling to straddle her hips. His shadowed face was harsh now, almost reverent.

"I've dreamed about you like this," he said, his voice a low rasp. "Almost every night since I met you. And then I'd wake up, and you'd be gone and I wouldn't know when I'd see you again." He paused, swallowing hard. "It was like dying a little bit. Every time."

God, this man touched her heart.

"You're stuck with me now," she said, an unexpected tear trailing down her temple. "We should probably make up for lost time."

"Damn straight."

Bending down, he caught her mouth with his, and she took him deep, opening for him so they could discover all the ways their lips and tongues fit together.

And then, too soon, he broke it off and leaned back again, out of range.

"I need to be inside you, Gloria. Now."

"Good. Hurry."

"I don't think I can go easy."

"Good," she said with a slow grin as seductive as she could make it. "Hurry."

"Why are you still wearing clothes?"

She started to lever up on her elbows so she could wiggle her way out of the dress, but he wasn't in a patient mood. Grabbing the two halves of the dress, he ripped them apart with a single hard yank, showering buttons and thread over the sheets. Half a second later, her bra got the same treatment, leaving her laid out before him.

He took his time with another slow perusal, his admiring gaze lingering on her small breasts and beaded dark nipples, which he cupped and stroked with his thumbs while she cooed with the raw pleasure of finally having his hands back on her body, where they belonged.

"I swear," he said on a shaky laugh, "you're the most beautiful thing I've ever seen. Ever will see."

Another wave of emotion hit her, making her tear up. Laughing and crying now, she swiped at her temple. "You couldn't make me any happier if you tried. You know that, right?"

"I still plan to try."

"Then make love to me. How about that?"

He eased down on top of her, giving her time to adjust to his weight and open her legs for him. Dipping his head, he took her mouth again, long and deep, and she tasted the salt of tears that weren't hers. And then, when she couldn't wait another second, he took his length in hand and stroked her wet core with the plump head of his penis.

She angled her hips, desperation getting the best of her, but he paused and raised his head, a question in his eyes.

"Go," she said.

With a single sharp thrust, he buried himself inside her. She cried out, her body adjusting to the delicious invasion, and his hands stroked up and down her sides and wedged their way under her butt, anchoring her as they found their rhythm together.

Panting, she stared up into his blazing eyes. Hung on to his biceps as they bulged with the weight of his body. Wrapped her legs around his waist and urged him deeper. Scratched his back with her nails. Nipped his throat and ears when he came close enough. Circled her hips and gave him everything she had.

His intent gaze never left her face as he made love to her like a man possessed, setting a hard pace that had them both dripping with sweat within minutes.

He murmured to her the whole time, words about how tight she was and how beautiful…how good she felt…how she was his now and he would never let her go.

How much he loved her.

She tried to answer back, but her heart was too full and she was too fascinated by the sight of their wet bodies twined together, her brown skin against his tan, their mingled sweat and cries. And she tried to hold off her orgasm, wanting this moment—this first time with Cooper—to last forever, but he relentlessly circled his hips and hit the exact right spot on her sensitized sex, and, really, she never had a chance.

Calling his name, she flew apart, arching into the pleasure as her body stiffened and went limp.

He took that as his cue, thrusting once…twice… three more times, and then he came with a hoarse shout, his head dropping into the hollow between her neck and shoulder as he collapsed on top of her.

Still inside her.

She hugged him closer, running her hands over his broad back and up into the ropy wet curls at his nape. Together they caught their breath, and then, just as she was on the edge of sleep, he shifted his weight, rearranging them both until he spooned her from behind.

She settled in, resting her butt against his crotch, and he rested one of his big hands on her breasts and the other on her sex, as if he wanted to make sure there was no question about who owned her body now.

His lips ran down the side of her neck, tickling her, and she grinned.

He held her tighter. "Marry me."

She stilled and held her breath, wanting to make sure she'd heard right. "I told you not to play."

His lips found their way to her ear this time. "Marry me. Put me out of my misery."

Drowning in joy, she let the laughter come. "Yes."

He grinned, the apple of his cheek scratching her with his five-o'clock shadow. "Where should we live?"

She thought about that.

"How's the big fixer-upper in Greenwich coming?"

"It's great." He nipped her ear. "Needs a woman's touch, though."

"I'm a woman."

"You certainly are," he agreed, stroking her breasts. "The neighborhood's got sidewalks. There's the beach. There's a big yard with a fence in case we want a dog."

"We want a dog!"

"We do?"

"Who doesn't?"

"I'm not into Chihuahuas and little purse dogs, though, Doc."

"Oh, God, no." She remembered a dog show she'd seen on TV a few months ago. "I want a Greater Swiss Mountain Dog."

"Hang on. Those things are a hundred and fifty pounds, aren't they?"

"Exactly! And they're beautiful and good-tempered."

"Good-tempered," he said thoughtfully, now twining his fingers with hers. "That's important. For when we have kids."

The image of sandy-haired, golden-skinned kids running around the yard, playing tag with a dog, made her smile. "Very important."

He nuzzled her neck. Cleared his throat.

"Could we have made a baby, Glo?"

That was when it hit her—they hadn't used condoms, nor had the idea even crossed her mind. And she wasn't on the Pill, because there hadn't been a man in her life in months.

"Yes," she admitted softly.

He grinned, his hand stroking between her legs becoming more purposeful. "Let's do it again," he said, nuzzling her neck. "Increase our odds."

"We can't," she protested weakly. "We have to get

ready for the rehearsal dinner soon. And I don't have a dress, do I?"

"We have a little time," he said, turning her in his arms and settling into the cradle between her legs again. "And as soon as we get a free minute, I'm going to marry you."

Chapter 15

There she was, Cooper thought the following morning, which was Talia and Tony's wedding day.

And his wedding day. His and Gloria's.

They were, in fact, already married. A trip to city hall at the crack o' dawn, a flurry of paperwork and a civil ceremony, with only a clerk and the photographer as witnesses, had seen to that. And now they would have a traditional Polynesian ceremony on a private beach miles away from the resort, because their marriage was just for them, and they certainly didn't want to steal any of Talia and Tony's thunder.

So they'd keep it quiet for now and thank their lucky stars that their attendance at the other wedding that day wasn't required until early that evening, giving them a little time to themselves.

Hanging on to the sides of the dugout canoe as his three bare-chested and red-sarong-wearing attendants, whose names he didn't know, rowed him ashore, he smiled at Gloria, who was already waiting for him on the beach. She looked amazing, of course, sun kissed, glowing and happy in her simple dress of white linen. They'd found their wedding clothes together, and he was also in white linen, although he was a little more flamboyant than she was, with a traditional red sash tied around his waist.

More male attendants provided their soundtrack, a thrilling and relentless staccato of drums. Island women in red-and-white flowered dresses danced for them. Another group of women in grass skirts were on standby, waiting to instruct them on the hula, and he was pretty sure a fire dancer would make an appearance later. Beside Gloria, the Tahitian priest waited to officiate, decorative spear in hand and an elaborate feathered headdress standing tall on his head, and the interpreter stood at his elbow, ready to explain the words to him and Gloria once the ceremony began.

They were observing every tradition they could because their wedding day, like his bride, was precious, and just because they'd arranged it quickly didn't mean they'd skimp on the details. A stunning feast was already laid out on palm fronds, waiting for them: roasted pig and chicken, raw tuna and mahimahi, lobster and shrimp, sticky rice, yams, a dozen different fruits, of which he only recognized watermelon, mango, pineapple, coconut and bananas—the selections went on forever.

He and Gloria would exchange fragrant red leis and leafy crowns made with the prettiest yellow flowers he'd ever seen. The priest would bless their simple wooden rings in a wooden bowl, bind their wrists with a leaf and then wrap them in a flowered Tahitian quilt to symbolize their unity.

All of it would be amazing, but to him there would never be anything as beautiful as the smile on Gloria's face as he climbed out of the canoe and walked barefoot down the powdery softness of the beach to stand by her side.

"Hi," he said, taking her hand as the drums reached their crescendo and the priest moved to stand in front of them.

"Hi."

His smile melted away. It was too much of a challenge to smile and breathe when she was looking at him like that. As though she could possibly love him a millionth as much as he loved her.

"You're beautiful," he told her.

"So are you."

"Let's get married."

"Cooper," Gloria said.

It was two hours later, after their wedding ceremony and feast. They'd changed back into their beach clothes—black linen for him and a fluttery blue sundress for her—and snuck back to the resort with no one the wiser. She could hardly believe their good fortune. Now it was past noon, which meant it was time to attend to Talia and Tony, who were, after all, the official wedding couple, and help them get ready for their ceremony tonight. Talia was already wondering where Gloria was and had texted her a couple of times. So she needed to say goodbye for now to her new husband and head over to Talia's bungalow for an afternoon of champagne-fueled pre-wedding pampering. There was no time for anything else.

"Cooper," she tried again.

He didn't answer.

Feeling breathless, she stared at her new husband's down-turned profile as he unlocked his bungalow door. His right hand moved with quick, sure movements. The fingers of his left hand were twined with hers, holding her in an unbreakable grip. His jawline was hard. Set. And his big body radiated a heat more powerful than the bonfire they'd just left.

"We don't have time—"

His gaze flicked up to her, a piercing glint of blue. Then he swung the door open, tugged her inside after him and nudged the door shut with his foot.

"Cooper."

To her utter astonishment, he raised her hand, flipped it over and pressed a kiss—oh, he was so gentle, so sweet—into her palm. His serrated breath fanned out across her skin, making nerve endings buzz with anticipation until she was dizzy with it.

Her gaze flickered up to his.

His face was wet. Tears glittered against his dark lashes, and his eyes...

His eyes were the most amazing things she could ever hope to see—diamonds and aquamarines.

And she was in love with him. Helplessly, hopelessly, breathlessly in love with him.

"I should probably tell you," he said softly, "that you're the best thing that's ever happened to me."

"That's funny. I was just thinking the exact same thing about you."

He tried for a rueful smile. Failed. Shrugged. Held her gaze. "I'm so in love with you," he said, his voice cracking. "You have no idea how much I love—"

He couldn't go on. With a choked sob, he murmured her name and pulled her into his arms. Need collected, hot and slick, between her thighs, and suddenly she was the needy one.

She gripped his prickly cheeks between her hands and stood on tiptoe. His mouth found hers. She yielded and took, opening to the salty sweep of his tongue even as she locked her arms around his neck and ran her fingers through his silky curls.

She needed him closer, so she scraped her nails across his scalp, urging him on. She needed more of his circling hips thrusting against her sweet spot, so she hooked one of her legs around his waist. She needed his two-handed grip on her ass to be harder, to hold her tighter, to never let her go.

"More," she gasped when his lips roved across her face, nuzzling her forehead and cheeks…her eyes, nose and neck. "I need more, Cooper. Don't stop."

Stopping seemed to be the very last thing on his mind. Breaking free, he jerked his tunic off, pausing to wipe his eyes with it before dropping it to the floor.

Then he reached for her.

Heavy lidded, she stared at him, this beautiful man she'd married. He was too thin now, and she planned to learn to cook for the sole purpose of fattening him up a little, but he was all broad-shouldered, taut-bellied sinew, as though he'd sprung to life from one of Michelangelo's sketches, and he was perfect.

And she wanted to taste him.

Shooting him a purposeful glance, she went to work on his belt.

"No," he said warily.

"I'm your wife now." She kicked off her shoes, dropped to her knees and pressed her face to the heavy bulge of his crotch so she could nuzzle him. His head fell back and she wanted to lick the golden column of his throat, to nip, to suck. His groan was a low, earthy rumble that fed every primitive impulse she had. "You can't tell me no."

Staring up the length of his body, she unzipped his fly, reached beneath his boxer briefs, took his thick penis in her firm grip and waited.

With a shuddering breath, he burrowed his fingers in her hair, angled her head way back and looked down into her face.

One of his tears dropped, splashing the corner of her mouth. She licked it, watching him.

"You're going to break me," he said, his voice so low and raspy she had to strain to hear. "You know that, don't you?"

"I don't want to break you," she murmured, knowing the heat of her breath against the head of his penis—it was a perfect plum now, swollen and ripe—

would drive him wild. Sure enough, his hips began to thrust involuntarily, and she tightened her grip. "I just want to own every part of you."

"You've owned me since I laid eyes on— *Gloria*."

She licked him, a long, lingering swipe up his length that culminated with a swirl—and a suck. He stiffened, his fingers tightening reflexively in her hair, and the near pain was sweet. Delicious. So was the strain to her mouth and tongue. She took him deeper, bobbing her head up and down...learning the feel of him in her mouth...the raw animalistic sound of him in her ears.

Until he couldn't take it anymore and wrenched free. Panting and wild-eyed now, he stared down at her for one glorious second.

Then he bent down, hauled her up by the arms and swung her around, ripping the covers out of the way before roughly tossing her to the bed. She landed on her back. By the time she'd finished bouncing, he'd joined her and reached under her dress for her panties. He jerked, she wriggled, and the panties hit the floor. She spread her legs, reaching for him, but he had other ideas.

Flipping onto his back, he pulled her astride him and latched on to her waist. She just had time to brace her hands on his chest before he entered her with a single powerful thrust that made them both cry out.

Then she began to move, swiveling her hips in wide circles and riding him hard.

They stared at each other the whole time, so she saw the way the sweat broke out across his forehead and upper lip…the way his wet eyes turned to sapphire…the way they glazed over as his body tensed… the way he struggled to keep his heavy lids open and watch her.

They spoke to each other, the same breathless mantra over and over again.

"Cooper."

"You don't know… You don't know how much I love you…. You don't…"

And then, when her thighs had started burning with the effort and she couldn't hold back the sensation any longer, she came in a piercing wave of pleasure so intense she actually saw black spots pop before her eyes. Sated and exhausted, she let her head fall back and her body go limp.

Beneath her, he stiffened, arching back into the pillow with a final groan. She stayed where she was until the tension eased out of his body. By that point, there was nothing left of her but rubbery spaghetti, so she toppled to one side of him and stretched out on her back.

Maybe she passed out. Maybe she slept a little.

The next thing she knew, there was a soft touch at her temple.

"Hmm," she said, smiling. "Cooper."

Opening her eyes, she discovered him lying next to her, smoothing her hair back from her face. He was right there, all wide eyes and rapt attention.

"What?" she asked, smoothing the line between his brows.

"I can't live without you," he said quietly. "Just… for the record. I can exist, but I can't live."

"Good." She ran the backs of her fingers across his lips, which were still swollen from her kisses. "Now you understand."

"Understand what?"

"How *I* feel. Why I married you."

The beginnings of a smile crinkled the corners of his eyes as he leaned in to kiss her.

Epilogue

"Look, husband, she's still crying." Talia, her face aglow with newly wedded bliss, nudged Tony with her elbow. Bride and groom looked down the candlelit table to Gloria, who was, in fact, pressing a linen handkerchief to her eyes. "Do you think she'll stop before they start with the toasts?"

Tony shook his head dubiously. "I don't know, wife. I thought they'd have to sedate her during the ceremony."

"Oh, very funny," Gloria snapped as they laughed at her. The reception, which was beneath a white tent on the beach, was in full swing, and the toasts, cake cutting and dancing would happen soon. "You two geniuses write your own vows, then you recite them without notes and you talk about how *your* health issues—" she pointed to Talia "—and *your* war experiences—" she pointed to Tony "—only made you stronger and love each other more, and then you expect the rest of us not to cry? Are you insane?"

"A couple discreet tears are one thing," Tony said, looking her up and down and shaking his head in mock dismay. "You're a mess."

"Now, look," Gloria said, laughing. "Just because you're family now doesn't mean I won't still hurt you. Just so you know. I still have my eye on you. You're still day-to-day as far as I'm concerned."

Tony raised a brow. "Day-to-day, eh? Man. And here I thought we'd bonded, Glo."

"Bonded?" Gloria cried. "Do I look like the bonding type?"

She glared at him. Tony looked crestfallen. Talia said nothing but looked worried.

Then they all burst out laughing. Further down the length of the table, someone clinked their champagne glass. More clinking ensued until the music stopped and the crowd's excited chattering died out.

Cooper stood, his glass in hand.

"Can I have your attention for a minute?" he asked. "Don't worry, Marc, I'm not cutting off the liquor. Just making a toast. No need to look so alarmed."

Marcus snorted. "Everyone who's ever heard you give a toast is looking alarmed."

Everyone laughed.

Talia took the opportunity to whisper in Gloria's ear, "So I notice that the wooden ring on your right hand matches the one on Cooper's right hand."

Gloria, who'd earlier noticed her sister's keen gaze on her newest piece of jewelry, was ready with evasions that weren't outright lies. "What, this? I found it this morning. Pretty, isn't it?"

Over at another table, Mr. Davies cupped his hands around his mouth. "Shut up and let your brother talk, dummy!" he called to Marcus, to more raucous laughter from the crowd.

"And did Cooper also get his ring this morning?" Talia continued in Gloria's ear. "I'm curious because they look an awful lot like traditional wedding bands. Tony and I thought about using them for our ceremony."

Gloria held her gaze and tried not to smile, which was hard when she was this happy. But her marriage to Cooper was precious and new, and she wasn't ready to share it with anyone just yet, including her sister.

And this was Tally's day.

"Wow," Gloria said. "Even on your wedding day, you find time to be nosy. Impressive."

Talia shot her a sidelong—and knowing—glare.

Tony slung his arm across the back of Talia's chair. "Are you two going to keep talking and miss the toast? Were you raised by wolves or what?"

"Shhh," Gloria said.

"Do I have everyone's attention now?" Cooper asked. "'Cause I've been working on this little speech, and it's pretty freaking brilliant. Everyone done with the yak-yak? Okay. Good. Here goes."

He took a deep breath, his gaze briefly flickering to Gloria, who flushed furiously.

"Mmm-hmm," Talia muttered.

"I don't know what you're talking about," Gloria said, then took a hasty sip of water.

"Some of you may have noticed," Cooper began, "that a change has come over the Davies men in the past couple years or so. My cousins Sandro and Tony, and my brother, Marcus, and I have all turned into fine men. Oh, sure, we were always handsome, smart, charming and kind to small animals—"

"And modest!" called Mrs. Davies.

"—and everyone but Sandro now showers at least once a day—"

Sandro had been bouncing his baby son, Pietr, on his lap while Skylar, his wife, looked on. Without missing a beat or looking away from his son's face, he raised a hand and gave Cooper the finger.

"Hey," cried Nikolas, Sandro's teenage son, whose hair was pumpkin-orange with black roots. "I saw that, man!"

Sandro shot the kid a narrow-eyed warning look. "You saw nothing. *Nothing.*"

"—so we're very proud of our progress since we were kids," Cooper went on. "And there was this one time when the four of us decided it would be a good idea to see if we could sail our rubber rafts from the Hamptons to Miami, so you know it was touch and go for us for a while."

"I remember that!" called Arianna, the younger sister of Sandro and Tony. "The folks had to call in the Coast Guard to bring your butts home!"

"Wow," chimed in Arianna's husband, Joshua,

who'd spent time in prison on a wrongful conviction. "And I thought *I* had a checkered past."

More laughter.

"But lately," Cooper said, "the Davies men have a new maturity. A new happiness. And, no, I'm not talking about the fact that the auction house landed Judah Cross's auction and made a killing on it."

Marcus and Claudia, who was now his wife, grinned at each other.

"No," Cooper said. "I'm talking about the women who've come into our lives."

Nikolas pulled a face and made gagging sounds. Sandro playfully smacked him on the back of the head.

Cooper ignored this disruption. "Sandro found his beautiful Skylar, a veterinarian who can handle the savage beast. And she's good with animals, too."

Everyone, including Sandro, laughed. Cooper raised his glass to Skylar, who inclined her head before kissing Sandro.

"My brother, Marcus, met his match in a spicy Brit who actually looks better in black than he does, and that's hard to do." Cooper raised his glass again. "To Claudia."

Claudia pressed a hand over her heart in thanks, then accepted a regal kiss on the cheek from Marcus. Both were wearing black linen amid the sea of white.

"And Tony." Here, Cooper got a little choked up and had to pause. Pressing his lips together, he held up a finger. "Give me a minute on this one."

Everyone clapped for encouragement.

"Take your time, Coop!" someone yelled.

Gloria swallowed back her latest surge of tears; Tony ducked his head; Talia ran her hand over his shoulders.

"We thought we'd lost Tony in the war," Cooper said. "And then he came back to us, but he was broken. And then he found Talia. Beautiful Talia. An artist whose glowing presence brightens our hearts the way her paintings brighten our walls. And now Tony's whole again, better than before. And I know that everyone here is praying, like I am, that Tony and Talia have sixty happy years together, because no one deserves it more. So..." He cleared his throat and raised his glass. "To Talia."

"To Talia," the crowd echoed.

By now the only pair of dry eyes in the house belonged to Talia, whose glorious smile was blinding, especially when Tony pulled her onto his lap and buried his face in her neck to hide his tears.

Gloria wiped her eyes.

"One last toast," Cooper said, his gaze now connecting with Gloria's. "I hope you don't mind if I paraphrase from Proverbs. To excellent wives, who are hard to find but who are more precious than jewels. The hearts of these men trust in you, and we will have no lack of gain." He paused, raising his glass to Gloria. "To our excellent wives."

"To our excellent wives," the crowd murmured.

Cooper sipped and lowered his glass, his gaze still locked on Gloria. *I love you,* he mouthed.

Gloria kissed her wooden wedding band, pressed

her hand over her heart and beamed at Cooper, her new husband.

I love you, she mouthed.

* * * * *

A sizzling new miniseries set in the wide-open spaces of Montana!

THE BROWARDS OF MONTANA
Passionate love in the West

JACQUELIN THOMAS	DARA GIRARD	HARMONY EVANS
KIMANI ROMANCE *Jacquelin Thomas* **Wrangling** WES	KIMANI ROMANCE *Dara Girard* **Engaging** BROOKE	KIMANI ROMANCE *Harmony Evans* **Loving** LANEY
WRANGLING WES	**ENGAGING BROOKE**	**LOVING LANEY**
Available April 2014	*Available May 2014*	*Available June 2014*

The newest title in the *Bayou Dreams* miniseries…

Forever's PROMISE

Fan-favorite author
Farrah Rochon

Between helping care for her nieces and running her recently opened coffee shop, Shayla Kirkland has no time for romance. Until she meets Xavier Wright, the hunky E.R. doctor who has the local females waiting in line. But how will Xavier offer her forever if he plans to leave town as soon as his work is done?

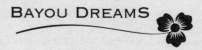

BAYOU DREAMS

"The heat from the two leads practically sets the pages on fire, but it's the believable dialogue and well-defined characters and storyline that make this novel a must-read."
—*RT Book Reviews* on *A FOREVER KIND OF LOVE*

Available April 2014 wherever books are sold!

HARLEQUIN®
www.Harlequin.com

KPFR3500414

He has long learned not to trust women…but then she came along.

KIMANI ROMANCE

TRUST
In Us

AlTonya Washington

Self-made developer Gage Vincent learned long ago not to believe the words of a beautiful woman. But he thought Alythia Duffy was different. Yet how can he trust her after he finds out that she is bidding for space in his hot new skyscraper? Will Alythia be able to prove to him that she is the special woman meant to share his life?

Available April 2014
wherever books are sold!

HARLEQUIN®
www.Harlequin.com

KPAW3510414

REQUEST YOUR FREE BOOKS!

2 FREE NOVELS PLUS 2 FREE GIFTS!

KIMANI™ ROMANCE

Love's ultimate destination!

Two classic full-length **Eaton** *novels in one volume!*

AWARD-WINNING AUTHOR
ROCHELLE ALERS

ALWAYS
AN EATON

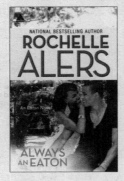

In *Sweet Dreams,* Denise Eaton, the scion of a Philadelphia dynasty, could lose everything. The man who holds the key to her future? None other than Rhett Ferrell, the man who broke her heart in college. Rhett has never forgotten Denise…and now he's vowing to steal her heart.

In *Twice the Temptation,* Chandra Eaton mistakenly leaves her journals—containing very private, very erotic dreams she's been having for the past two years—in a Philly taxicab. Her embarrassment turns to intrigue when Preston Tucker finds and returns them. And that's when things *really* get interesting….

"This one's a page-turner with a very satisfying conclusion."
—RT Book Reviews on Secret Vows

Available April 2014 wherever books are sold!

www.Harlequin.com

A poignant tale of longing, secrets and second chances.

LIBERTY

GINGER JAMISON

When Ryan Beecher returns home after a long deployment overseas, Lexy barely recognizes her husband. The cruel and abusive soldier who left is now a gentle, caring, tender man—one suffering from amnesia, with no memory of her or their life together. And his touch awakens yearnings she's never felt before. Can Lexy trust this lover, who seems to live only for her pleasure…as he seeks his salvation in her healing embrace?

Available now wherever books are sold!